BOTS

THE UNCANNY VALLEY

Nicole M. Taylor

EPIC
Press

The Uncanny Valley
Bots: Book #3

Written by Nicole M. Taylor

Copyright © 2016 by Abdo Consulting Group, Inc.

Published by EPIC Press™
PO Box 398166
Minneapolis, MN 55439

Cover design by Dorothy Toth
Images for cover art obtained from iStockPhoto.com
Edited by Jennifer Skogen

Library of Congress Cataloging-in-Publication Data

Taylor, Nicole M.
The uncanny valley / Nicole M. Taylor.
p. cm. — (Bots ; #3)
Summary: SennTech rolls out its latest and finest creation, a Hart-style Bot
who can see individual DNA signatures, and she's got her sights on Edmond West.
Meanwhile, hostile forces are converging on the little island
where Edmond and Hart are hiding.
ISBN 978-1-68076-003-3 (hardcover)
1. Robots—Fiction. 2. Robotics—Fiction. 3. Young adult fiction. I. Title.
[Fic]—dc23
2015932713

EPICPRESS.COM

"The Uncanny Valley": *Def. The hypothesis that as a non-human object grows increasingly humanoid and realistic, the small imperfections are emphasized, causing revulsion. A well-known problem in robotics.*

ONE

THE CHILDREN'S ROOM

PALO ALTO, CALIFORNIA. FEBRUARY, 2045

"All of this must be very different from what you are used to." The woman—Gina—was chittering like a bird. She reminded Kadence of a bird, in fact. Not one of those large, colorful birds that demanded attention with their size and luster, but something more like a sparrow. Unobtrusive and all in shades of beige and slate. Gina was clearly a nervous talker and she was just as clearly very nervous right now.

Kadence didn't think of herself as a particularly intimidating presence, but every time Gina turned to her, she looked as though she expected to be back-handed at any moment. She and Gina had communicated primarily via instant message and one brief phone call. Kadence didn't have much to go on, but she had expected someone a bit more assertive. Presumably, Gina did this sort of thing all the time, right?

"It's . . . um . . . it's not that different," Kadence offered, feeling as though she should at least say something in the face of such naked vulnerability. She was lying, of course.

At the lab, there had always been a very specific set of rules guiding the creation and development of the Bots. Janelle had insisted on a "statistically accurate representation of the United States of America." Which meant, roughly, an even gender split and a strong showing for various minority groups.

Here in the bowels of SennTech's corporate office, Kadence could not help but notice a preponderance of female Bots. Many of them had an ethnically neutral face with any obvious racial characteristics softened, like a cartoon illustration. And they were, each and every one of them, gorgeous.

That element wasn't, in and of itself, so different from the military labs. There had actually been a number of meetings about the unrealistic attractiveness of the Bots as a whole. Kadence herself had read a series of awkwardly-worded memos on the subject. How, exactly, might some middle-manager tell a bunch of lab rats to please make their AIs less distractingly hot?

They did have a point, actually. Some of the earliest models were so perfectly symmetrical, their faces and bodies so devoid of flaws that they had something of the living doll about them. Kadence had seen them when they came back into the lab for cosmetic modification. It was, frankly, creepy. Over time, the Bots had grown more human but ultimately no less beautiful.

Kadence chalked it up to simple human impulse. If you could make something more aesthetically pleasing, wouldn't you? And so it was that the average roomful of Bots was simply more attractive than the average roomful of humans, designed as they were by boring, unthinking evolution.

But the SennTech creations were another thing entirely. Kadence thought that this must be what wandering backstage at a fashion week event felt like. These willowy yet voluptuous figures, these perfect jaws and luxuriant manes of hair. It felt almost obscene just to be looking at them, as though she were peeping at someone in their underpants. As she moved amongst them, Kadence was acutely aware of her own flaws—the weight that settled disproportionately in her hips, the raised bump at the top of her nose, her thin, yellow hair.

For all her general timidity, Gina the guide seemed unfazed by the situation. Perhaps she had simply become inured to it over time. Or, perhaps, despite her gun-shy demeanor (not to mention her adult acne), she was actually very self-confident.

"You're looking at our bulk models here," she said, waving a hand at a passing Bot (tall, limpid eyes, large breasts). "We have other limited edition lines for more eclectic tastes."

Kadence could not help but look after the Bot who brushed past the two of them with seemingly zero interest. Somehow, the engineers had managed to mostly avoid that unnerving sensation that one was looking at a creature rather than a person. The guide noticed Kadence's stare. She smiled slightly.

"We have the finest aesthetics development department in the world." There was just the tiniest hint of smugness in her voice.

Kadence actually doubted that. Not because SennTech didn't have the means and motive to procure such people but because, from all that she had seen, Edmond West was the best Bot designer in the world. It had taken her months to earn the privilege of looking at his original files, all his specs on the very first Hart Series, and it had been a humbling experience. There was a naturalism to her that Kadence had yet to see in anything that had come out of the military lab, let alone SennTech's demonstrably inferior production department.

But it would be impolite to bring that up.

Kadence had learned that talking about Dr. West was not done in the military labs and she suspected that there might be a similar unspoken rule here. After all, West had run out on his nebulous (though, from what Kadence understood, legally binding) contract with SennTech as well. Their future might have been very different had he stuck around and built a commercial Bot fleet for them as he had promised.

Kadence, at least, would have had a very different life.

"We're very pleased with the excellent progress we've made in terms of synthetics. Now we're hoping to step it up in the realm of cognitive architecture."

Despite all the precautions that the military had taken, rumors of the Hart Series Bots had surfaced almost the moment the first Hart Series went into the field. SennTech must have been furious; the technology that West had promised them was now the sole and protected property of the US Army. It would be years before SennTech got their hands on a Hart Series and, by then, the floor would be open to any other enterprising company or individual.

There was, of course, a silver lining to that particular storm cloud. In the wake of West's defection, the robotics development division had become much less of a one-man show. Hart Series Bots were being manufactured in greater and greater numbers, an enterprise that necessitated more techs, more designers, more thinkers, and more grunts. A million little fissures that an enterprising person— or company—could exploit.

"We hear you are the finest cognitive architects in the field," Gina beamed.

Cognitive architects. When was Gina going to stop pretending that was an actual term that people used? And Kadence wasn't, in fact, the finest thing-that-doesn't-exist. That would probably be Hector, at least amongst her cohort. All of them worked in the shadow of West himself.

Kadence was much more of a communications person—she knew how to make synthetics talk. Sing, if she flattered herself. But she knew her way around a Bot brain and, most importantly, she knew how a Hart Series was made from beginning to end. That was something neither Gina nor SennTech would ever specifically ask her for, but it was what they wanted all the same. Kadence didn't care about the semantics, though, as long as they came through on the promised compensation.

She had now been silent for a very long time, Kadence realized. Gina was looking up at Kadence, her face radiant with expectation. Kadence nodded deeply and made an agreeable sort of noise in the back of her throat. She hoped that would suffice.

Gina's smile shrank ever so slightly. She seemed very aware of Kadence's discomfort. Then she made a thoroughly unexpected move; she reached out and took Kadence's hand. Kadence allowed this, letting her hand rest limp and inert inside the other woman's.

Gina looked first to one side of them and then to the other, like a cartoon character about to divulge a secret. "Shall I show you something special?" she asked conspiratorially.

". . . Sure," Kadence said slowly. "Yes. Do that," she added, with more conviction. All of this cloak and dagger bullshit, it wasn't for her. She wasn't an international spy, she was just a science geek who had gotten lucky with an internship.

When she had agreed to come on board with the military's robotics program, it seemed like all her dreams were coming true. An outstanding student at an unremarkable school, she knew she had big fish syndrome and she fully expected to get knocked on her ass by the competitive job market. But the Army bigwigs had seen something in her and the weapons development assignment was the first step towards a secure career in her field. True, the pay was barely existent, but it wouldn't be that way forever and she was young and strong, she could scrounge for a little while. If things got really bad, she could always count on her parents for support. They weren't rich but they were solidly middle class and they had never hesitated to bail out their oldest girl, the family's highflier.

That was before the doctor's found a cloudy little white spot on her fifty-six-year-old father's MRI. A lesion, one of many in the tender white matter of his brain. Kadence had studied brains like that before; brains afflicted with Multiple Sclerosis. So, when they called to tell her the news, Kadence knew what had happened before her mother even finished explaining, halting, stumbling a little over the unfamiliar medical terms.

And suddenly it seemed that money, which had been such a small part of her life before, was all she could see. Even after securing a full-time position at the lab and a commensurate pay raise, it wasn't enough. It wouldn't ever be enough. Her father's disease was debilitating and long-term. Kadence might have twenty more years of hospitals, tests, treatments, and caretakers to finance.

Last year, her father had to bow out of the construction business he'd spent fourteen years building. He couldn't trust his increasingly numb and clumsy hands and he had started to experience psychiatric problems. Kadence had to talk her mother out of quitting her own job (a receptionist for the local high school) to care for him.

Kadence had herself added on to the majority of their financial accounts so she could monitor them and pay what bills she could. And so her parents weren't forced to say certain things to her face, things like, "We're losing the house."

She wasn't arrogant enough to think that she was the first person that SennTech had approached. That probably would have been Golden Girl Eun-hye or else Hector the Studious Grinder. But she was the most desperate, and that made her desirable in an entirely different way.

What she didn't understand was why SennTech

insisted upon pretending to "court" her. As though her compliance was predicated upon seeing their Bots in the habitat they had designed for them or hearing all about SennTech's marvelous vision for the future. But, Kadence supposed, she was their creature now and it behooved her to act like it.

And so she followed dutifully along as Gina led her into an elevator. "We keep them on the top floor," Gina said conversationally as the elevator thrummed along. "They like the view." Kadence doubted that. She had never known a Bot to care about the sort of things that preoccupied humans.

The elevator's interior was paneled with dark, reflective glass. Kadence stared at her shadow self in the door. The tint of the glass made her lips look purple and her skin look teak. Her eyes suddenly seemed huge in her face, as though she had just witnessed something horrible and it had left her stunned.

Gina wasn't lying about the top floor, the elevator didn't stop until they reached the thirty-fourth floor (really the thirty-third because SennTech was apparently superstitious about the number thirteen).

Kadence heard them before she saw them, a chorus of high-pitched, lute-like voices reciting something together in near-perfect unison.

"Are those children?" Kadence asked. Gina nodded, her eyes sparkling with enthusiasm.

"Yes! You see, this is where SennTech really sets itself apart in the artificial intelligence field."

Kadence decided not to point out that virtually any private corporation with access to Bot technology would almost certainly begin manufacturing ChildBots in great numbers. Catering to pedophiles may have been ethically distasteful but, economically, it just made sense. Pedos were quite literally a captive audience, and ChildBots were their only legal option for sexual expression. Manufacturers could bleed the motherfuckers dry and who was going to complain?

Kadence even figured someone like Gina could develop some sort of human-rights pitch about it, like they were saving real children by supplying synthetic ones. From what she'd heard about Edmond West, he'd had a similar idea with the original Hart Series.

Kadence herself had no opinion about all of this. She had long ago decided that the ways in which people used the Bots was no concern of hers. A person could go crazy thinking like that, like they were responsible for all the evil in the world. And Kadence had enough to get on with just keeping herself and her family afloat, she could not afford to spend too much time on the woes of other people.

Despite all of this, Kadence wasn't really prepared for the experience of actually interacting with a ChildBot. As Gina led her towards the open room where the voices spilled out, Kadence found herself unaccountably anxious. It was as though she were being led to some unknown punishment and it made her feel oddly childlike herself.

The room itself was cheerful but sterile, like a

half-decorated day care. There was a big, old-fashioned chalkboard along one wall with nothing written on it. There were roughly a dozen ChildBots of varying ages, everything from toddlers on unsteady legs to young women, probably the equivalent of a human fifteen- or sixteen-year-old. The gender split was scrupulously even and their faces were just as cherubically lovely as the adult models. It was somehow less jarring on a child, however, as human children tended to be cuter on the whole without the familiar flaws and heaviness of adult faces. They all wore the same informal uniform as the other Adult Bots: a dark, long-sleeved shirt and loose-fitting pants. It managed somehow to look awkward on all of them, regardless of height or size.

The majority of them were sitting on a colorful carpet, facing towards an Adult Bot who was paging through an illustrated book. Occasionally, she would tap the book's page and blow up a specific image so the children could see it clearly. A few other children milled around the room on seemingly unrelated errands. One or two sat alone, interacting intensely with some colorful toy. Several of them looked up when Gina and Kadence entered the room.

Kadence only barely suppressed a shiver when the Bot children turned their faces towards her. Adorable though the faces may have been, they evinced the same odd, flattened characteristics that the adult Bots did. It was peculiarly alarming on a miniature body.

And, like all Bots, they had that disinterested, faraway look in their eyes. Kadence wondered if that expression was a major factor in the development of the Hart Series. No matter how useful the earlier generations of Bots were, no matter how indisputably safer they were, they would always be the "creepier" option. Kadence wondered what it was like, interacting every day with these not-human things that looked so much like humans. They seemed to mill around freely in the offices. Unlike the military labs where the Bots were kept in designated areas, one might encounter one of their odd, synthetic faces anytime they turned a corner. Maybe that was why Gina was so relentlessly upbeat?

"Emily," Gina said, curling her finger in a "come-hither" gesture at a girl of roughly ten or eleven. A Bot girl made to look like a ten- or eleven-year-old, Kadence corrected herself. Technically, she was probably less than a year old.

She had long brown hair and there was a little bit of wariness commingled with the studied blankness of her face. Her eyes were just a bit too far apart, making her look like a visitor from another planet. That was the first thing that Kadence would fix. Also, she might change her teeth. They were strong and white and perfect; a girl that age should have a few small dental defects for realism.

"Emily represents our greatest step towards a more sophisticated iteration of the SennTech humanoids," Gina said, putting her hands on the girl's shoulders like a proud mom. It was true that there was something different about Emily. A depth that the other Bots didn't appear to have. She returned Kadence's scrutiny with a steady gaze.

"Hello Emily," Kadence said finally, reaching out a hand for the girl to shake.

After what seemed like a very long time but was probably only a few seconds, Emily took the proffered hand. "Hello," she said, her voice clear and sharp. She sounded older than she appeared. That was also something that would have to be corrected. "You're the one who is going to upgrade me." It was hard to tell whether this was a statement or a question.

Kadence looked from Gina to the girl and back again. "Yes," she said. "I'm going to be your Blue Fairy," she added, a sudden flash of inspiration. Kadence didn't know exactly why she'd said it, it was hardly the moment for a joke and neither of them seemed like they had great senses of humor.

Emily just looked at her, uncomprehending.

Apparently Pinocchio wasn't on the syllabus here at SennTech U.

"Thank you, Emily," Gina said smoothly, dismissing the girl with a smile. Emily drifted back across the room, to a low shelf bristling with more picture books.

"So," Gina grinned, "what do you think?" Kadence realized what the little woman reminded her of: the teacher's pet who always got straight A's impatiently awaiting some test result.

Truthfully, Kadence had expected to develop the SennTech version of the Hart Series from scratch. She hadn't expected to do it via a series of upgrades, but she supposed that made sense. Perhaps it had something to do with property rights? If SennTech could legitimately claim that their Hart Series were actually a modified version of their existing AIs, maybe they could avoid the military bringing suit against them.

Of course, considering all the trouble that the Army was currently seeing with the Hart Series

Bots, suing for patent claims didn't seem very high on the to-do list. Kadence wondered how much SennTech really knew about the Hart Series's tendency to go rogue when out in the field? They'd have a real problem if a bunch of their synthetic "wives" started telling customers to get fucked.

But Kadence wasn't in charge of customer satisfaction. She was contracted to build them a better Bot and that's exactly what she would do. They could discover the drawbacks as they went, just as the military had.

"She's an excellent start." Kadence smiled and found it improbably difficult.

Gina gave her a hearty slap on the back, a move Kadence associated with old businessmen, not petite young women. "Kadence, I'm so glad you're coming on board. I think you are going to fit right in to the SennTech family." The little woman beamed at her as though there were no single person in the world whom she valued more.

"Of course," Kadence mumbled, unable to look her in the eye.

"And of course," Gina said, snapping back into a professional posture, "we'll make sure to get that signing bonus over to you ASAP."

Kadence smiled at her and, for the first time since she had walked through the doors of SennTech's offices, it was utterly genuine.

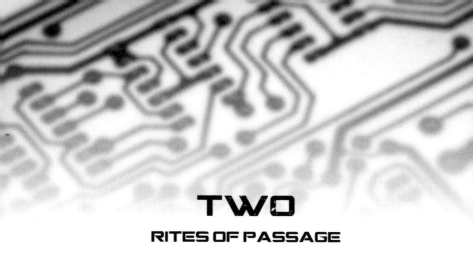

TWO

RITES OF PASSAGE

First, Hart gave herself bangs. Then she gave herself a menstrual cycle.

She performed both of these operations with a similar cautious precision in the small, lone bathroom at the cabin. She did not announce her intentions to Edmond, nor did she specifically attempt to hide her DIY upgrades. She half-expected him to knock on the door and ask after her when it became clear that she was going to spend a protracted amount of time shut up in the bathroom.

But no knock came.

When she emerged the first time (after the

bangs) she found him huddled in the bed with all of the extra bedding in the house heaped upon him. He looked to her like a picture she had seen in an online encyclopedia—a bear, preparing for hibernation. The bear was grossly fat and guarded, tucking its face away in its ample belly.

But in Edmond's case, it was only the blankets that added heft to him. He had been growing thinner and thinner ever since they left the farm. Hart was unsure how to address this problem. She supposed that he must be eating because he left the remnants of containers and wrappers in the trash and, periodically, she found freshly-scrubbed dishes in the little enamel sink, but she rarely saw him do it.

Once or twice, Hart had tried eating along with him, but it was a supremely awkward experience. Their meals had little of the charm of other foodstuffs she had tried. Beans and rice with a minimum of seasonings. Edmond was, he told her, not much of a cook. Hart understood in the abstract how to follow a recipe and produce a finished dish but she struggled with any element of improvisation. She could not do anything "to taste."

The beans and rice seemed to form a single gluey mass that stuck in her throat unpleasantly. Most of her plate went back into the pot which was then transferred into the round-edged refrigerator that Edmond said was on its last legs.

Edmond ate more than she did, but barely. Ingesting the food allowed Hart to develop a nutrient profile for the meal. She estimated that Edmond had consumed approximately 800 calories per day. Someone of his height and (healthy) weight should really be eating somewhere in the range of 1,900 to 2,500. His face had developed a slight indentation just below his cheekbones and extending down towards his mouth. It made him look like he was frowning even when his mouth was objectively neutral. It made him look older. Though Hart supposed that he was older than when she had first been activated. Each day, his cells died and only some of them regenerated.

She wondered if he was attempting to make the food last as long as possible to spare them a potentially dangerous trip into town. That was a poor plan, if that was, indeed, his plan. At this kind of caloric deficit, his body would soon begin consuming itself.

That was an idea that never failed to boggle Hart. That a human could devour itself from the inside out, leaving just the bones like a particularly assiduous scavenger. At least that was one weakness that Edmond had not passed on to her. Provided her internal components remained steadfast, she would never require additional nutrition from food or water. Her life was electric, wireless, chemical, genetic. She breathed for the appearance of breath, not for the want of air.

When they did need to go into town, it was fuel that drove them there, not food. The cabin was heated with a squat wood-burning stove. The warmest place in the house was directly in front of the glowing red grate and they propped all the doors open so the heat would radiate out to other parts of the house.

Hart didn't have much to compare it to, but she could not remember ever having been cold in the laboratory. On the farm, they had lived in a low, rectangular house made of light-beige metal. Edmond told her it was called a trailer home. There, heated air gusted up through metal vents in the carpeted floor. But it was much colder in Michigan.

Here, they had to feed the stove tree cuttings, and the few bundles of firewood they had taken from the convenience store were hardly enough to last through the first week. Cold was an interesting proposition for Hart. She had not been designed or programmed with any sort of temperature regulation and so she was, just like a human, subject to the whims of the elements. She would be very unlikely to die of cold, even fairly extreme cold, but it did give her considerable discomfort. There were many days when she and Edmond did not move from a place in front of the stove, wrapped in big blankets and swaying towards one another like trees with co-mingled roots. Hart had discovered that Edmond produced considerably more body heat than she did. She was, on average, seven to ten degrees cooler than he was.

"That's your skeletal infrastructure," Edmond said. It was one of the rare times when he consented to speak specifically about her development as a machine. Mostly, he seemed uncomfortable with any questions in that vein, as though he were attempting to pretend that she had simply sprung forth, fully formed, from the earth itself.

Instead of circling back to the convenience store, which Edmond said was surely the scene of considerable scrutiny by various unknown authorities, they decided to try for the next town, twenty-eight miles to the north.

It was right along the edge of a lake. Edmond didn't know what the lake was called and Hart didn't either. In her mind, she named it Applestem Lake for the thin little fissure of a canal that extended out from the top of the lake and into the town. It was almost entirely frozen over except for a few dark gray spots far out in the middle.

There was a small grocery store there and a handful of restaurants, mainly offering variations on freshwater fish. There was a rummage-y catch-all store with rocks glinting in the windows. That store was closed, Hart knew, because she had drawn up close to the window to inspect the wares.

"It's a geode," Edmond told her, when he noticed how she stared at one specific stone, halved to reveal a heart full of purplish protrusions. "The inside is mineral crystals. That one looks like amethyst."

There were very few people in town. She and Edmond strolled up and down the aisles in the grocery store and their footfalls seemed unusually loud against the backdrop of muzzy music from the store's sound system.

The only other people in the store were a pair of women. Or rather, a woman and a child. In her travels (which, admittedly, had been minimal) she had discovered a curious quality of human development: how terribly individualized it all was. The girl (Hart supposed she must be a young girl from the way the older woman addressed her) was almost physically indistinguishable from an adult. She was tall and broad and she had a round, disagreeable face. Hart wondered if she herself looked older than the girl, who had certainly existed on the earth much longer than Hart had.

The girl and (Hart assumed) her mother stood in front of the hair care section, staring at a display of cardboard boxes with smiling women on the covers. In front of each box there was a little loop of colored thread or fabric. Every once in a while, the mother would reach out to point at one of those loops.

On the other side of the aisle, Edmond was examining the bar soap, undoubtedly looking for the most inexpensive option. Hart drifted away from him and over to the mother and daughter. She hoped she looked casual and uninterested in their conversation.

"Mom, I told you fifty times, I want red," the girl hissed.

"That is red," her mother countered. She flicked one of the little loops and, up close, Hart could see that it was actually hair. She wondered if it was from a real person. The hair the older woman pointed at was reddish-brown, a woodsy, autumnal color that made Hart think of dying leaves.

"That's barely different than my regular color." The girl grabbed the ends of her own hair and waved them at her mother. She was correct; her hair was brown, somewhere between Pantone 1605 and 167. The box the mother had selected seemed only a few shades warmer.

"That's good, it'll be a subtle change."

The girl gave a massive eye-roll, as though that were the most absurd thing she had ever heard anyone say. "I don't want subtle. I want that." She pointed at another box entirely. The attendant loop of hair on that one was a raging, inorganic red, like a stoplight.

The mother let out a sigh. "You'll look like a goddamned tomato."

The girl whirled around to face her. "It's not your hair, it's mine! What do you care, anyway?"

Perhaps the mother had just noticed Hart in that moment or perhaps she simply wanted a smooth exit from a difficult conversation, but she looked over her daughter's head at Hart and said, "Sweetie, move aside, this woman wants to look."

The girl looked at Hart as though she had intruded on something private and shuffled away towards the sticky pomades. She was still talking to her mother, but her voice was just an irritable mutter now.

Hart stood alone now in front of the wall of

what she knew to be hair coloring kits. The display went from darkest to lightest and there clearly wasn't much of a market for people with dark hair in this town, because there were only a handful of black hair dyes, all the way down at the bottom. Hart crouched down, inspecting each box. One was the same color as her own hair. She reached out and touched the loop in front of the box. It felt strong and smooth, like woven silk. Her own hair was coarser than that, she gritted it between her thumb and forefinger to make sure.

Undoubtedly, that texture was encoded somewhere amongst the multitude of genetic markers that Edmond had used in his physical construction of her. She had not asked him—and she didn't think she ever would ask him—why he made the choices he did. Why dark hair? Why gray eyes? Why her freckles? Why the two moles, like a fanged bite, just underneath her shoulder blade? He was so meticulous, each one of those decisions must have had some sort of extensive thought process behind it. At some point, he must have decided that everything from her double-jointed thumbs to the wild single curl in her eyebrow offered some significant advantage to an organism.

"Hey," Edmond said softly, wheeling the cart over to her. "What are you looking at?"

Hart wasn't sure. "This hair . . . it's very soft."

"It's probably doll hair," Edmond told her. "I don't think they'd waste real human hair on this sort of thing."

"Doll hair is texturally different?" Hart got to her feet, still staring down at the box. The woman on the front smiled shyly, her profile turned towards the viewer. Her hair, like a sheet, enfolded her upper body.

"Well, yes. It's just a synthetic."

While she had been observing the mother and daughter, Edmond had filled the cart with several gallons of distilled water and bundles of firewood. Underneath the cart, he had loaded the metal rack there with even more wood. It looked to be about an eighth of a cord. Hart calculated that the load would offer them approximately two more weeks of heating, if they were prudent. Perhaps they would need to return. Hart didn't know how long Edmond wanted to stay in Little Rick's cabin. She suspected that he himself could not answer that question for her.

When they got to the checkout line, Edmond pulled out his crumpled white envelope and handed over some of the last few bills to the attendant. If they did come back, they would have to find another source of cash.

While Edmond paid, Hart loaded their scanty purchases back into the cart. Behind Edmond, the mother and daughter approached the moving belt. The girl was holding a box of hair coloring, that vivid red. She set it down on the belt with an air of challenge, though her mother behind her looked only resigned.

Briefly, the mother looked up and caught Hart's eye. The expression on her face was entirely opaque.

"Just you wait," she said suddenly. Hart almost laughed to see Edmond start and look around him, as though there might be someone else that she was addressing. The woman continued to stare right at Hart. "Just wait until you have one of your own."

———o———

Edmond had not made her hair. At least, not her hair as it existed in its present form. He had developed a code for what her hair could theoretically become but Hart was bald when she was activated. She remembered clearly the strangely pleasant sensation of soft prickles of hair making their way through the skin of her head slowly, over time. For Hart, it was a discovery every time she encountered a mirror but Edmond must have had some sense of what it would become. What she would become.

At first, Hart had been very content to become

what Edmond designed her to be. To express his code in synthetic flesh and imitation bone. Increasingly, however, it felt unnecessary for Hart to hew so closely to choices Edmond had made, seemingly to her own detriment.

Why, for instance, had Edmond made her so relatively weak when she could potentially be so strong? Why had he made her vulnerable to bullets and blades, just like any human person? She was capable of so much more. Why had he confined her to the kiddie pool, evolutionarily speaking? She had not asked these things of Edmond. At first, it was because she was a little afraid of what she might hear. She had an inkling of the kind of existence that Edmond had intended for her and she didn't need or want to hear that from his lips.

But now, she couldn't help but think that she didn't need an answer from Edmond. Because she could answer her own questions. It didn't matter why he had crafted her weak if she could change herself to become strong. Code determined the color and texture of her hair but the world was full of tools for modifying oneself. And, while Edmond may hold the intellectual copyright to all of Hart's components, she was the sum of her parts and she only belonged to herself.

Her hair was hers as well.

The scissors (which she had found in a sticky little drawer in the kitchen) were spotted with orangey rust. They were difficult to open and close, but Hart had no better option. Using her fingers, she brushed her long hair over her face so that it fell equally from a swirling point at the top of her head. She looked at herself in the little bathroom mirror as though through a widow's black veil. She drew her hand down the hank of hair in the front, holding it tight and straight, slightly away from her forehead as she lifted her other hand for the cut.

The scissors were unwieldy and her first pass left a few scattered strands of uncut hair drooping awkwardly amongst their shorn fellows. Hart gave it a second try and it wasn't perfectly even and the right side was definitely lower than the left, but she supposed it was the best she could do with the tools she had.

Edmond said nothing about her experiment for several days. Then, as she was feeding logs into the stove one morning, he said to her with a meditative air, "Next time, if you like, I can cut it for you."

Hart couldn't deny the utility of that idea. With a second pair of eyes and hands, the cut would almost certainly be more precise. Nevertheless, she felt in some way protective of her awkward new bangs. It wasn't that her hair gave her any particular aesthetic pleasure but rather that it was an outwardly visible change to her body that had been made by no one but herself. From now on, Hart wanted to be the one holding the scissors.

"No," Hart told him. "I don't need you for that."

When it came to changing her insides, however, the process was considerably more complicated.

It wasn't actually the first time Hart had made alterations to what she increasingly thought of as her "default settings." Before they had left the lab, she had experimented with increasing her strength, stamina, and, critically, pain resistance. As it turned out, all of this was for the best. She had needed every one of her enhancements to get the two of them safely away from the base. Even then, she had nearly powered down and had to be rescued by Edmond's own blood. It was a ridiculously inefficient system, this flesh and blood. Who would choose this, if they had a choice?

But, in the lab, she had access to the full array of tools and tech that Edmond had used to create her. Here in this wintry forest, she barely had the things necessary to make a birdhouse. What she did have, what she carried with her everywhere, were the raw materials. Hart was, after all, made of herself.

Edmond's innovative use of encoded stem cells meant that, in theory, Hart could redirect any of her cells to serve whatever purpose she desired. And, right then, Hart wanted to bleed. Or rather, she wanted to menstruate, which was not something she had thought much about before. Not that she'd had a great deal of time for deep thoughts on such matters. It often seemed to Hart that, despite the inarguably short amount of time since she had been activated, she had lived a great deal. She had certainly stacked up a tall pile of events, all of which deserved a thorough parsing all their own. Perhaps she would be allowed the time to do that thinking, someday.

It was, of course, the woman in the grocery store who had kicked off this idea in Hart's head. The woman in the grocery store and, perhaps a little bit, the dead girl whose pyre still stood, black and insectile, in the snow behind the cabin. That girl was of an age to start menstruating, but she never would. Even if she had not deactivated on that country store floor, she would not have been given a functioning reproductive system. What possible use could it have been to her, a girl that would never become a woman anyway?

Hart knew about menarche, the first onset of the regular bleeding that would give cyclical structure to most women's lives. She had read all about it during one of her research tours of the Internet. Hart knew a lot, generally speaking, about human development. She found it both fascinating and frustrating. It seemed to her an unforgivably slow process by which one was introduced to their adult body. She had come into the world fully formed, already mature. She would never know what it felt like to be a child and she would never feel the awkward pangs of the in-between stages. She had never thought of this as a loss before but it suddenly seemed to her that there could be something worth knowing, something that she couldn't glean from a flex-tablet but must taste and touch and feel.

She could not, of course, simply rewind her body

to some prepubescent state that never, technically, existed. Her marvelous cells, capable of so much, had no memory of smaller bones, differently arrayed flesh, more rudimentary brain synapses. She was now as she had always been, would always be, perhaps.

In addition to the purely biological details of the phenomenon, Hart had also read about the multitude of cultural practices that centered around menstruation. Whether a culture considered this blood sacred or profane, whether they engaged in ritualized washing or lavish celebrations, one thing seemed constant: menarche was a clear designation between child and woman, a line of demarcation that the male of the species apparently lacked.

There was a surety in that which appealed to Hart. It was an objective metric by which one could measure the otherwise utterly oblique transformation from child to adult.

Hart scraped her raw materials from the outside of her left thigh. Using the ancient set of knives from the kitchen, she eventually removed a three-inch-by-three-inch rough square of her skin, so thin that the light shone right through it. With any luck, she could turn this patch from dermal tissue to endometrial tissue and transplant it into her uterus. It was a matter of reprogramming her cells and instructing them upon their new identity via compatible code.

As for getting the tissue inside her body, well, there was really only one way to do that.

Again, Hart quarantined herself in the bathroom. The bathtub was, she decided, the only reasonable place she could perform this surgery. She jury-rigged an old plastic hand mirror against the water faucet so she could clearly see her lower abdomen where she had drawn directions in black permanent marker.

She lowered herself into the tub, which was much shorter than she was. She crawled her feet up the tiled wall until her spine was flat against the bottom. It was porcelain and cold but she knew that her skin would warm it soon.

It wasn't until she had made that first cut and saw, after a moment of trepidation, the shockingly red blood burble out, that she realized it was entirely possible that she had no womb at all. After all, Edmond had no intention or desire to make her in any way fertile. Maybe instead of designing her reproductive system to be inhospitable to life he had simply skipped the entire apparatus?

There was only one way to know. And Hart was thankful again that she had adjusted her pain tolerance.

It was still uncomfortable, of course, and there was a strange pressure and a sensation of something foreign working inside her. She cut as delicately as possible—endless shallow slices—through skin and subcutaneous fat until she reached something hard and slick. She touched it with her wet fingers. There it was, a tense and powerful muscle, as complete as the rest of her. Hart could not help but smile.

Of course Edmond had made every single part of her and made each one as perfect as possible. She should have expected no less from a craftsman of his caliber.

In the mirror, Hart marveled at her own interior. It was a vivid strata of color, dull ashes-of-roses pink, shocking white, burnt reds, and always the alarming crimson of her fresh blood. She had a sudden desire to see the rest of herself, turn herself inside out, if she must. She wanted to know the smallest things inside her body and how each of them worked. She wanted a full mastery of everything that she was.

She applied the graft to the wall of the uterus, where it clung easily. In a few days, possibly a few weeks, she would know if her experiment had been a success. She stitched the incision closed with what was left of the medical thread that Edmond had purchased back in California. She patted the closed wound after wiping away the excess blood. Her body was fully capable of forming scars,

Edmond had seen to that. Perhaps this would leave a reminder on her skin.

In the days that followed, Hart tried to determine whether she felt in any way different. She felt a sense of foreboding, or at least a sense of something oncoming. But perhaps that was only her own expectation.

Once again, Edmond had nothing to say about her project, though she suspected that, this time at least, it was because he had sensed no change in her. He would not see the telltale red line on her belly, he would not touch her there and feel the little pinpricks of stitches. But if her behavior seemed inconstant or bizarre, he had nothing to say about it.

He had nothing much to say in general.

It snowed the day that Hart's experiment was complete. It snowed most days, of course, but this storm was particularly potent. The high winds had blown a lot of the existing snow into huge, impassible drifts around the exterior of the cabin.

Later, they would shovel it away, not with a snow shovel, but with an ordinary metal one that transferred all of the cold up into their unprotected hands.

Hart, who almost never emitted waste, recognized that something was different because of a sense of pressure or fullness in her belly. She couldn't suppress a little frisson of excitement as she ran to examine herself in the privacy of the bathroom. Sure enough, a trickle of blood emerged from her body like a red tear.

Hart smiled to herself and almost immediately frowned. She had expected it to feel like . . . something more. An announcement or a magic trick. She expected to feel the way she had during the surgery, when she was opened like a flower and full of working, moving parts. That sense of discovery and of wonder was what she was hoping for. And this was just blood.

It was possibly the most human of human things, and here she was, unmoved.

Her bangs were longer now. They fell into her eyes until she tucked them behind her ears, where they became indistinguishable from the rest of her hair. And now this wasted blood, neither celebrated nor scorned. Unnoticed, in fact.

She would have to find some other way to become a woman.

THREE

MEMORIAL

He did not give her permission to mutilate herself.

In general, Hiram Liao thought that he communicated fairly well with his daughter, Shannon. She called and texted regularly and responded to his logistical e-mails in a timely fashion. She even visited approximately once every three months.

This had been part of their agreement. He would finance Shannon's undergraduate degree as long as she promised to do a few important things. She had to major in something actually applicable to the real world (she had chosen linguistics); she had to maintain her strong academic performance, of course; she had to actually complete her studies; and she had to stay in contact with her old father. He thought that these rules were fairly innocuous and he had not wanted to overload her with strictures, but now, Hiram realized, he should have added something about not puncturing holes in herself.

He had not noticed the LEDs at first, bundled as she was in a puffy winter jacket. The past five years had been the coldest on record for California, and San Francisco was especially frigid, with its proximity to the Bay. The lights were clearly visible through the fabric of her t-shirt, however. Liao caught glimpses of them, winking like stars, as she dropped her bags and rifled through the kitchen cupboards. Whatever it was, it appeared to run just below her collarbone in a straight horizontal line.

After a cursory inspection of the house (as though anything had changed since her last visit), she darted down the stairs to the basement where she wasted no time stuffing her laundry into the machine.

"Don't they have machines in your dorm?" Liao asked her. Most of the luggage she had brought appeared to be filled with clothes in need of washing.

"They cost two seventy-five a load!" Shannon protested, grinning at him. It suddenly occurred to him that, three years before, she had still worn braces on her teeth.

"How admirably frugal of you."

Shannon just shook her head at him. She had cut her hair as well, and it fluffed wildly around her ears. He didn't like it. "Thanks, Dad," she muttered, not without affection, as she expertly picked her whites out of the load.

Nora had been devastated when Shannon was a toddler and the doctor had advised Nora to have a full hysterectomy in an attempt to dodge the cancer that had claimed both her mother and aunt. Hiram's wife was an only child herself and she had always wanted a big, boisterous family. Hiram had never told her so but, secretly, he was pleased that they would only have one child. He had four brothers and a sister and he didn't think the competition for resources had done him any particular favors.

Instead, they were able to lavish all of their time and attention on just one daughter. They had enough money to afford her every opportunity for success and they had the emotional energy to put her needs at the forefront of their lives. To him, it was just basic economics. But he could not deny a certain level of sadness when he saw Nora interact with the children of others. There was such a wistfulness in her, as though her very flesh and bone ached for them.

It seemed particularly cruel in retrospect, as the hysterectomy had not, in fact, saved Nora from her mother's fate. Perhaps it would have been better to wait, to have more children for Nora to love, albeit likely for fewer years. If it were a simple choice between children and Nora, Hiram knew exactly what he would decide. He loved his head-strong daughter, but he would easily trade all of fatherhood even for just a few more years as a husband. But that was the kind of fruitless calculation that people made in the midst of their grief, as if there were any bargaining power left to them.

"Remember to wash everything on cool," he warned his daughter. "And air dry all your delicates."

Shannon wrinkled her nose. It was something she had done since she was a baby, one of the first voluntary motions she had made. "Ew. Don't say 'delicates,' Bàba." She shooed him up the stairs with a flap of her hand.

———o———

Apart from clean laundry, Shannon always wanted one thing from her visit home: a trip to Hong Kong Palace, the family's go-to dim sum restaurant since before Shannon was born. She liked it partially because it had remained more or less unchanged for the last two decades. It was still owned by the same family, though the couple's grown son did most of the work these days and his now-elderly parents rarely put in an appearance. Even the fish in the big tank by the cash register looked almost identical to the ones that Shannon used to trace with a single finger when she was just a small girl.

She also claimed they had the best egg tarts in the world.

Over brunch, she told him about the handful of internships she was applying to for the fall. "What about you guys?" she asked, spinning the Lazy Susan at the center of the table until the plate of pork steam buns faced her. "Are there any programs for linguistics undergrads?"

After Nora died, Hiram couldn't count the number of well-meaning people who suggested that he hadn't really lost his wife because Shannon was a piece of her, still right here with him. In truth, Shannon wasn't much like Nora. She wasn't very much like Hiram either. Nora was reserved, almost cripplingly shy, in fact. Hiram was brusque.

Shannon had taken a third path, a gregarious class clown who fed giddily upon social interaction and fretted wildly in its absence.

He knew fairly early in her life that a career in the military would never work for her. Hiram's father, who had captained a submarine before he retired, was very proud when his son followed in his footsteps. But when it came to his own daughter, Hiram had no desire to enfold her in what had become a kind of de facto family business.

"Not really," he said. "Although that is not exactly my department."

Shannon nodded ruefully, as though she had expected this type of answer.

"You know, the school got a grant to put a bunch of those SennTech Bots on campus, did you see that?" she asked, not looking at him.

Shannon knew generally what Hiram did with the Army, but they rarely discussed it in detail. Primarily because there was so little about it that Hiram actually could legally disclose to her. He was very thankful that despite the on-going shit-show that the Hart Series rollout had become, the press had not yet linked his name to the project. Still, Shannon was a smart girl and likely knew that he had some knowledge of the development of advanced AIs.

"No," he said mildly, "I hadn't heard about that. What are they doing?"

Shannon shrugged. "Various things. There are even a few SennTech TAs. I haven't had any, though."

Hiram made a noncommittal noise. For a long moment, neither of them spoke. "They can do almost anything, huh?" Shannon said finally, sounding uncharacteristically disingenuous.

"People are always overly optimistic about any new technology," Liao answered.

Then the tea came and he occupied himself with pouring cups for the two of them.

"Are you going to visit Māma while you're here?" Liao asked and Shannon's manner changed.

She still seemed uncomfortable but in a distinctly different, more familiar fashion.

"Maybe," she said. As far as Hiram knew, Shannon had not been to Nora's grave since the funeral, almost one year ago now.

"I don't have much time," she added, prompted by Hiram's blandly disappointed look. "I have to be back on campus by Sunday night because I have a meeting with the Study Abroad people."

From there, the conversation drifted into shallower waters, safer and warmer. They talked about her potential study abroad plans (privately Hiram wondered whether or not she was expecting him to pay for these excursions) and her extracurriculars. In high school, Shannon had been the editor of the yearbook, a pole-vaulter, and a regular in all the school plays, but she had struggled to find her niche in college.

"I've been going to a couple of language labs. Pashto, mostly. It's probably good for me but it's not much fun, you know?"

Hiram was not surprised to hear that a roomful of undergraduates babbling awkwardly at one another wasn't exactly a thrilling way to spend a Saturday. Shannon had probably already outstripped the majority of them. She had always been quick to pick up languages. She learned Spanish in elementary school, of course, and by the time she was eleven, her Mandarin was already better than Hiram's, mainly because she had a much larger vocabulary. Hiram had what he thought of as "household Chinese," the language of his youth which he had largely abandoned by adulthood. Shannon had studied it avidly, however. She had even requested to attend Chinese school on the weekends.

In high school, she took Hindi as an elective, which opened up the wider world of languages from the Indian subcontinent. She spoke a smattering of Urdu and was learning Farsi now, apparently. More than anything else, though, she had discovered a love for the logic problem of language. Human development intertwined with a kind of musical interpretive quality. Liao approved of the change in direction. He always thought Shannon would make a fine academic. It was the sort of career that he had always wanted for her, somewhat cloistered, perhaps, but safe and steady and far removed from the worst of rat-race excesses.

"Oh!" she snapped her fingers as though the idea had just occurred to her, but Shannon was a bad liar and Hiram was very good at sussing out liars, bad or otherwise. "That's something they do. The SennTechs. They have them doing interpretive services."

She looked at him sidelong, as though gauging his reaction. He, of course, had no reaction. Nora used to tease him about his ability to turn a stone face on the world. "No one can tell what you are thinking," she told him. "Except for me."

"I don't know about that," she said softly, picking at her plate. "Bots as interpreters. But they say they're very effective."

"Undoubtedly," Hiram answered.

" . . . More effective than humans?" Shannon's whole face became a question, her eyebrows shooting up towards her hairline. It was an expression that Hiram knew well. Nora had done the same thing. It was as though they imagined that, if they threw their whole body into asking a question, then he would be bound to answer it honestly.

Liao had extensive anti-interrogation training, not to mention a not-inconsiderable amount of firsthand experience in the field. He wasn't going to be broken by a nineteen-year-old girl with a mouth full of steam bun.

"As I understand it, the SennTech Bots are the epitome of machine translation. But they lack an ability to reason and contextualize language as a human being could. So yes, more effective in some situations but still less effective in others."

Shannon chewed on this (and a bite of steam bun) for a long moment. "That's not what I heard," she said, taking a sip of water and looking coolly at him. "I heard they have a contextual sensitivity on par with a real person. I heard that, in a few years, they'd make human translation and interpretation obsolete."

Ah. There it was. The various language departments were undoubtedly having a mass panic attack at the idea of being muscled out of a job by a legion of tireless, uncomplaining Bots. Naturally, this was all filtering down to the students and, equally naturally, Shannon was worried about her own future career.

"But it won't affect you," Hiram pointed out. "You aren't planning to be an interpreter anyway. Bots will never be capable of the kind of advanced academic study of language mechanics that you're going to do." He offered her one of his rare smiles. "You are irreplaceable."

Shannon laughed, it had a little of the derisive snort in it as well, but she had flushed a bit and Liao knew that she was pleased with his assessment of her. Nora had been so good at telling Shannon that she was loved. Nora treasured the girl and it was clear for anyone to see. Hiram, on the other hand, had always struggled with that aspect of fatherhood. His instinct was not to say that he loved her or that he was proud of her. As far as he was concerned, that sort of thing should be taken as a given.

Instead, he focused on the practicalities of raising a daughter. He carefully researched everything from her first car seat to her first car to make sure that he was getting the safest and most cost-effective option. He took time to teach her skills like how to navigate a city by creating a mental map or how to perform basic household repairs. He paid attention to her interests and preferences. Never, in her nineteen years, had he ever gotten her the wrong flavor of birthday cake or a poorly received Christmas present. It seemed to him that if he did all of these things—and did them well—then no child should have cause to complain that they went unloved.

In all of these ways, he demonstrated daily how much he valued her. These were things his own parents had either been unwilling or unable to do for him, after all. But he knew that there was value in the words, like a talisman. Nora herself had told him often enough, "Sometimes, it's just good to hear you say it."

---○---

The notification came that evening when they were sitting in the living room, a companionable silence. The both of them were browsing their flex-tablets. Shannon had half-wrapped hers around her wrist and she held it up to her eye line as though preparing to ward off a blow. She tilted it expertly away from her father so the the images and text on screen blurred uselessly.

Hiram was using his flex-tablet in the more traditional fashion, albeit on a secondary, more secure network than the house wifi that Shannon used. In general, he did not like to check work communications while Shannon was present but, given the delicate situation, it was unavoidable.

Liao had earmarked this weekend for his daughter weeks ago, long before they'd gotten even an inkling of where Edmond West might be holed up this time. Then, two days before she arrived, they had received intelligence indicating that West and the original Hart Series had hunkered down on an island off the coast of Mexico. The source was allegedly a good one, but Liao was requesting double and triple checks. The United States and Mexico always had an uneasy relationship but, with the recent flare-ups over the Southern California Desalination Project, things were especially tense.

There was no question of going the legal route. Mexico would not extradite someone like West, not even if they declassified enough information to charge him with something. Plus, West would be in the wind before the Army filed a brief. They had lost his trail more than once because they paused to work out the logistics of moving in on him.

If they waited too long, they risked West moving on or someone discovering who he was and what he had. There were any number of groups in and around Mexico who would love to snatch up such a high-value target. But, if they went in over this information only to discover that it wasn't West at all, Liao's ass would be in a sling. No matter how they did this one, it was going to be noticed by Mexican officials. Probably by more than a few non-officials as well. If they were going accept that eventuality and absorb the consequences, the payoff had to be certain and absolute.

The e-mail arrived just as Liao was checking his mailbox. It was a flex-tablet photo and from far away, but Liao recognized West right away. He had lost weight and his hair had grown into a wild mass of curls, but it was clearly him. Liao's memory of the Hart Series was more hazy; he had only actually seen her a handful of times, but the woman with West fit her general description. Tallish, dark-haired, average build. He was certain of West and reasonably confident of the Hart Series. It added up to a rubber stamp of approval.

But an operation would have to start almost immediately. They needed to develop a plan and gather a team before arranging logistics. All of this needed to be done quickly and accurately. Liao also knew that he would have to spearhead this work.

The smash-and-grab plan was not a great favorite with the top brass. They had unanimously urged Liao to simply raze the island with a series of remote strikes. That plan also had the benefit of offering at least the thinnest veneer of plausible deniability. A training exercise gone bad or something like that. Equipment failures were always a viable option. Taking West alive, by contrast, was so risky and so labor intensive, and it was virtually impossible to innocently explain. Actual boots on the ground always made less sense than some impersonal error from the stratosphere. Liao had been able to convince them of West's ongoing utility to the project but he knew that, without his presence, they would likely fall back upon their more conservative instincts.

Ironically, it was West's little rebellion that had actually done the most work to convince Liao that he should be recaptured at all costs. The next generation of Hart Series, which he had been leaking into the outside world, were clear improvements upon the existing models. They evinced all of the artistry and innovation that had made Liao offer his card to the boy all those years ago.

If he could make those machines now, on the run with limited resources, imagine what he could do at a state-of-the-art lab with years to work?

Liao was confident that, with the correct balance of stick and carrot, West could be convinced to continue his work. In fact, Liao didn't think he'd be able to resist the lure of creation, not if his activities in exile were any indication.

Hiram looked over the top of his flex-tablet at his daughter. She was fully absorbed in her own machine, occasionally tapping on the surface impatiently. He didn't like the idea of leaving her here alone on one of her rare visits, but there didn't seem to be any other option.

"Shannon," he said, "would you mind terribly if I stepped out for a few hours?" In reality, he would probably be gone until the next day, at the earliest. But he suspected that Shannon would be asleep long before that happened. It was just as it had been when Shannon was a little girl; he ate dinner with the family, or tucked her in tight, and if he was gone in the intervening hours, who was to know?

Shannon didn't look up from her wrist. "Sure. Can I borrow Māma's car, then?"

He still hadn't gotten around to selling it, the little sedan they called the green-eyed monster. It was a cool mint color and Nora had loved it. It rested inert now in the single-car garage while

Hiram parked his own car on the street. No one had driven it since Nora died.

"Where are you going?" he asked.

At last, Shannon looked up at him. "Some friends of mine are down the peninsula. I was going to go meet up with them."

Liao wondered if she was, on some level, relieved that he was leaving her to her own devices. He wondered if the same wasn't true for him.

"Yes," he said, "you may use the car. But be safe. If you're going to drink—"

Shannon rolled her eyes hugely.

"If you're going to drink, use the self-driving feature, okay?"

"Yes, Dad, I know." This was the conversational foxtrot the two of them had danced regularly since she got her license. Each of them knew their part.

Shannon unfurled the flex-tablet from her wrist and stood up. Liao joined her, grabbing his own tablet. Together, they made their way towards the vestibule to retrieve their keys and coats and boots.

Shannon grabbed her purse from the post and hooked it over one shoulder. She dug out a tube of what looked like lip gloss and applied it without looking. Through her shirt, the lights in her skin twinkled at him. It looked like a Christmas decoration.

Hiram cleared his throat, uncertain. He pointed at her throat. "What's that?" he asked.

Shannon's eyes widened. She looked down at her sweater as though there were a stain somewhere on it. "Oh," she said finally, with a little laugh. She tugged the collar of her sweater down to reveal what must be a thoroughly healed dermal implant. Four little bulbs of light sat on top of her skin, anchored invisibly underneath her flesh. They flashed red, yellow, green, blue on a regular schedule.

"It's Māma's heartbeat," Shannon said, her voice soft. "From her EKG."

Nora's heartbeat. Hiram had listened to it a thousand times, with his head on her chest. It was steady and slow, as sweet as she was. He had not recognized it on the EKG, a cold, prickly line that jutted up and down with no particular purpose. And he hadn't recognized it in light, resting just inches above his daughter's own heart. Her young, strong heart that was sure to beat on for years to come.

Hiram enfolded his daughter in a hug. "If I am not back before you have to leave," he said to her, "it was very good to see you."

Shannon faced away from him, though he could imagine the look of tolerant amusement on her face. "It was good to see you too, Bàba," she said, very gently.

Together, they walked out of the home that had once belonged to the both of them, into the rain and the night.

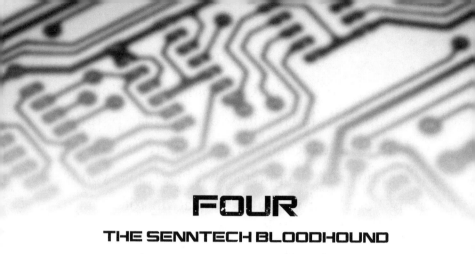

FOUR

THE SENNTECH BLOODHOUND

NORTHERN CALIFORNIA. MARCH, 2045

This was the first Bot that Kadence had developed nearly from start to finish, all on her own. It wasn't perfect. West, Janelle, even Hector probably could have done better, or at least have avoided some of her more costly and time-consuming mistakes. For all that, she was very proud of what she had done with Emily, the most advanced AI to come from the SennTech corporation.

That didn't mean, however, that she thought Emily was ready for fieldwork.

She wished that the Powers That Be would send someone other than Gina to liaise with her. It was impossible to argue with Gina in any meaningful way. The little woman just turned her smile up a few degrees and nodded as though she were taking in everything Kadence was saying. And then Gina ignored her completely and did whatever she was planning to do from the beginning.

Nevertheless, Kadence brought her concerns up again and again in the vain hopes of changing someone's mind.

"It's not about Emily specifically," Kadence said, "I would oppose the use of any ChildBot for something like this. It's just not practical. An unaccompanied child is always going to raise suspicion."

"Certainly, certainly," Gina smiled. "And we are hearing your concerns. But time is of the essence here and, as you well know, Emily is by far our most capable unit."

Kadence couldn't help but puff up a bit under such praise. Emily was a standout. No other SennTech creation could match her for intuitiveness, emotional intelligence, and even her visual appeal. After Kadence's intervention, she looked, acted, and spoke like a real human girl. She was just as good as any Hart Series—in some ways, maybe even a bit better. There were certainly some features Kadence had added to her programming that she knew full well were not in wide use by the military yet.

"She is very capable, but do you really think that she can do what the entire US Army hasn't been able to do?" Kadence pointed out.

"They haven't sent the entire Army after West." Gina seemed to be deliberately missing the point. "And the Army doesn't know everything that we know."

Gina said those sort of things occasionally. Little cryptic bon mots that suggested that SennTech had some working knowledge of where Edmond West was or where he was going to be. They had never told Kadence explicitly whether or not this was the case, probably to ensure that she had no useful information to offer the military should she decide to become a triple agent.

Triple agent. She couldn't even think that with a straight face. Kadence wasn't an agent at all, she was a scientist. In theory, she shouldn't care what they did with Emily after her work was done. But it frustrated her to no end because it seemed like such a waste.

"And what if she finds them?" Kadence said. "What then?" Emily was much stronger than any human child but she was still no match for the original Hart Series which was, as far as anyone knew, still traveling with Edmond. And who knows what other modifications West had made since then? In fact, who was to say that West and the Hart Series were alone? He could have surrounded himself with a Bot army by now. Was tiny Emily supposed to just grab Edmond by the collar and haul him back across the country, beating down opposing Bots at every turn? The idea was patently absurd, a suicide mission for what they claimed was their very best

Bot, the jewel in the crown, the asset that was to be protected above all others.

Gina clicked her tongue at Kadence, as though admonishing a small child. "Not everything is about brute force," she said. "Emily has so many other applicable skills."

———o———

The mods were coming in a fire hydrant stream, sometimes three or four in a single day. But still Emily kept track of each one. Every week, she would export her data to Dr. DeSouza and wait for the awkward blonde woman to tell her everything she already knew about the impact of each addition, subtraction, streamlining, and junking. Dr. DeSouza insisted on doing this with her, though Emily had assured her that it was unnecessary. "I have time," Dr. DeSouza always said and Emily had time as well. At night, she went back over her modifications, feeling out the new expanse of herself.

It was mod 37-D that made Emily extraordinarily sensitive to trace or touch DNA on various surfaces. It was followed shortly thereafter by mod 37-E, which allowed her to focus on one or two DNA profiles at any one time. Those miserable hours before the subsequent mod, when she could sense every instance of trace DNA on any surface she encountered were brain-bruising. Each of the profiles overlaid the others and commingled, she felt like a balloon too filled with water, stretched thin with the task of containing. It was the first time she had cried. It was the first time that she remembered, at least.

There were many things that Emily could not remember.

Dr. DeSouza apologized for this on several occasions. "If I had been here from the beginning . . . " she would say but she would not complete that sentence. Dr. DeSouza was the most apologetic of the doctors. Most of them didn't talk to Emily at all.

When the doctors came in to import Edmond West's genetic profile to her central computer (which Dr. DeSouza was always encouraging her to simply call her mind), none of them said anything to her. They maneuvered her as though she were a particularly large and posable doll.

Except once. One time they did say something to her: "You are the world's leading expert in Edmond West," they said.

Emily had never met Edmond West. She had never even seen a photograph of him. From his genetic code, she could develop a visual profile of him that was likely to be between 97 and 98 percent accurate. More than enough to pick him out on a busy street. But she could only guess at certain gene expressions, not to mention any sort of personal style he might have adopted. Emily was not comfortable with guessing.

That was why she had requested access to

Edmond West's social media accounts and to his various e-mail services. The social media was largely a dead end. Most of them had only the most cursory biographical information and nothing that might reveal his thought process or inner life.

The e-mails were better, but they were still brief and largely concerned with logistics. Edmond was practical, single-minded to the point of myopic. He was prone to depression and, while very intelligent, he was also arrogant. So arrogant that he probably hadn't even noticed it.

Of course, only someone very assured of their own tremendous intelligence would have dared to do what West had done. Unleash the Hart Series Bots and then attempt to take them back, as though the world would simply accept his sincere apology and erase the last few years of technological history.

It pleased Emily to know that Edmond West had not made her. She was a SennTech creation, similar but not the same. She was distinct from this man and his suffocating ego. They said he had brought his first creation with him. Hart was said to be the most realistic of the Bots, the most expressive and the most intelligent but Emily could not imagine that she would have entirely escaped the flaws of her creator.

When they sent her out into the world (the first time she had left the SennTech commercial building since she was just a series of components) they outfitted her lightly. They gave her a flex-tablet, albeit with limited internet access. It was to be primarily a communication device, so she could check in with the doctors at regular intervals. It was also loaded with a generous amount of funds in the wallet application, enough to pay for transportation services and lodging services, should she require them.

Emily did not think she would require them. Edmond West had to sleep and she didn't and she was loath to give up that kind of advantage unless it was strictly necessary.

Transportation was a trickier idea. The fastest

thing to do would be to get a car somehow, but, as a child, Emily would not be permitted to do so. SennTech had corporate cars, of course, but she was sure to attract attention, a small girl behind the wheel of a flashy car. In truth, Emily wasn't entirely sure that her legs were long enough to operate the pedals correctly. Self-driving cars were a possibility, but they still legally required a licensed driver to be present.

And then there was the issue of optimum functioning. Emily wasn't at all sure that she would be able to detect trace amounts of West's DNA from a moving vehicle. She had always practiced at a slow speed, usually moving under her own power and Emily did not like the idea of introducing an unknown variable into the situation when it was at its most critical.

Thus, her chariot of choice: a chunky mountain bike with a stripe of electric purple that wound around and around the center aluminum bar. Purple was Emily's favorite and she was very pleased to have found a bike that featured the color.

————o————

She started in the Lake Piney region, inland and north of the Oregon border, far from SennTech headquarters in Palo Alto. This was where SennTech had determined Edmond West was squatting on an illegal marijuana farm. Emily found traces of him all along the route. On a gas station pump handle, sprayed over a ditch full of high grasses, on the glass door of a small town grocery store.

As Emily approached the farm itself, she started to pick up an interacting set of DNA profiles that appeared with considerable regularity. She focused in on them: four men, two women, five dogs. Two of the men were white, one Latino, and one mixed race, Black and Latino. One of the women was white, the other likely Hawaiian, though Emily conceded that she could also potentially be Native American. Three of the dogs were Rottweilers, one was a small terrier mixed with beagle, the last was a Chow-Chow.

Emily used the long, uninterrupted time on her rides to develop visual profiles for all them. A short, brunette woman with a bulb on the end of her nose, a man with a high forehead and minty green eyes, a regal Chow with a black-splattered tongue.

In a strange way, she was almost excited to meet them. She rode severnty-four miles to them and, over those miles, they had become like figures from a fairytale that she had heard of, night after night.

She met the dogs first, or one of them at least. The terrier mix, wire-haired and muddy, it appeared like an apparition from the edge of the trees. It had been raining on and off all day, which was why Emily hadn't sensed the animal's approach. The dog quickly made itself heard, however, barking caustically at her as it skittered amongst the trees.

The dog never left the treeline, but it tracked her, running parallel to her bicycle as Emily made her way down the road, which was really just a worn-in two-track. Emily had an odd sensation then, one she had never had before, not even just before the doctors came to perform another modification. She was feeling fear.

Not of the terrier itself, though it continued to shrilly protest her presence, but of the other dogs that she knew would be along shortly. It was irrational fear. No dog, not even the Chow, could puncture her skin or break her bones. That had been another modification.

Sure enough, Emily rounded a curve that took her deeper into the forest and there were two of the Rottweilers and the Chow. He was redder than she imagined, like a sunset, and though his fur was damp from the rain, there was something majestic about him.

The three of them stood in the road, blocking her path. They were not overtly threatening, the terrier had ceased his barking and none of the other dogs deigned to growl or bare their teeth. Instead they were simply very still and immutable, like an impassible wall made of fur and teeth and button-black eyes.

Emily slowed her bike and then stopped it entirely about four feet in front of them. She dismounted carefully, putting down the kickstand behind her. She stretched out her hands in front of her, palms open and empty.

"See?" she said, "I'm okay."

The dogs did not move.

Emily took one step towards them. And then another. Still no reaction. She was drawing very close now, almost close enough to touch one of the Rottweilers, a female. Though she had seen some scattered wildlife on her long journey, Emily had never physically touched an animal, let alone a dog, before. Suddenly, she had the urge to feel the dog's fur and know the texture with her fingers the way she knew it with her mind.

And then something very strange happened. Just as she reached out for the dog's glossy black head, it began to emit a high, frightened whine. It did not move or snap, it seemed frozen. But still that sound, escaping from closed purple lips and clenched white teeth. It was afraid, extremely afraid. Of her.

She looked over at the others. They were all afraid of her. That's why they were stopped stark in the middle of the road, that's why they did not attack her. For the second time in less than hour, Emily found herself experiencing a totally alien sensation. Something about this idea, that dogs would fear her, made her . . . uncomfortable? Unhappy, perhaps?

She did not have time to analyze this feeling further, because it was then that a tall woman appeared, clomping through the trees and crackling branches as she went. She wasn't showing anything, but Emily strongly suspected she had a weapon on her. It was the Hawaiian or possibly Native American woman. Her hair was piled up on the top of her head and she was wearing a cheap green rain slicker, the kind that was little more than a tarp with a head hole cut in it.

Her face was suspicious, but it softened with

confusion when she saw Emily. "Hey, kid," she said, "this isn't a through road. It's all private property back here."

Emily didn't speak. This was her moment of truth, the first time she had interacted with a human outside of SennTech. This would determine whether or not she could legitimately pass for a real person. A real girl.

What would a girl say now?

"People hunt back here," the woman continued, "it's not safe."

"I . . . got lost," Emily managed, finally. "And I saw the dogs."

The woman seemed to notice the dogs for the first time. She wrinkled her eyebrows as though their posture and behavior were unusual to her as well. She made a clicking noise with her tongue against her teeth. "C'mon guys," she said, slapping her hand to her thigh. The Rottweilers and the terrier obeyed, loping immediately to her side. Only the Chow remained. His head came up to the middle of Emily's rib cage and he looked steadily at her.

If he could talk, Emily thought suddenly, I would be in trouble.

"Bingo," the woman said, more insistently. "Come!"

The Chow obeyed, though slowly and with obvious reluctance. He took up a place in front of his mistress, between her and Emily. The woman reached out to scratch behind the enormous dog's ear and looked thoughtfully from the animal to Emily and back again.

"Where were you going that you wound up here?" she asked, a little hint of suspicion creeping back into her voice.

"I was looking for my sister," Emily said. That wasn't the cover story she had planned. She had not, in fact, planned a cover story at all. The doctors had assured her that her appearance as a harmless child would be enough to forestall most serious questioning. "She said she was gonna be here for a while. She's with this guy, tall, curly brown hair. Kinda nerdy."

The woman appeared to be digesting her words.

"This is my property," the woman pronounced finally, "and your sister isn't here."

Emily nodded soberly. "Okay, I'll just go back the other way, then."

The woman said nothing and just stood there, watching as Emily returned to her bike and climbed back on the seat. The doctors had said that people would trust her, that they would not be wary of someone who looked like a child. She wasn't sure exactly what to do in this particular situation.

Emily was strong, she could probably overpower the woman, even if she did have a gun. The dogs were unpredictable, their desire to protect their owner might win out over their fear of Emily. If she took that route, she would have to follow through completely. She would have to kill the woman and the dogs, possibly the other people as well.

If she did that, however, she would still be no

closer to Edmond West. What she really needed was to get access to the farm and see if she could pick up a trail there. And, for that, she needed the woman to trust her, at least enough to offer her some minor hospitality.

Tears were still something of a novelty to Emily. She had only been capable of physically producing them for a period of weeks, part of mod 42-F. Initially, she found it difficult to summon them, she squeezed her eyes together and made a noise that she thought approximated a sob. But then, as she hunched over the bicycle, her hands tight on the bars, she began to feel a real swelling of emotion inside her. She allowed that melange of feeling—confusion, frustration, fear—to overtake her. And finally, wetness sprouted from her eyes like mushrooms after a rainstorm.

"I . . . I don't know where to go," she sobbed, hunched over the bike. "My sister is supposed to take care of me and I . . . l-l-l-lost her!" She allowed her voice to become a howl. The dogs cocked their heads at her.

The woman looked uncomfortable, which was much better than suspicious. "Uh . . . " she started to step forward and then stepped back, an awkward little dance. " . . . I don't . . . " Her lower lip bent downwards.

"Okay," she said finally, "you can come back to the house. Does your sister have a tablet or a phone? Can you call her?"

Liquid was coming out of Emily's nose. Was that a part of crying as well? Being a human child was a thoroughly unsettling affair. "Yes," she sniffed, "I can call her."

The woman led her through the forest, the dogs keeping a cautious distance. Emily noticed that one side of the woman's poncho hung uneven, as though there something heavy in the pocket on that side. Emily walked her bike slowly over felled branches and piles of leaves. Thus far, she wasn't getting any new DNA signatures, except for the ever-present samples from wild animals, which she easily filtered out.

The house occupied a small clearing that had apparently been created very recently. There were stumps littered around the yard, still with fresh white sawdust piled on top of them. It was a small-ish trailer, trimmed in blue with a rickety set of wooden stairs, which looked homemade.

The woman ushered her inside quickly, the dogs crowding in after them. The actual grow fields were probably further in but Emily didn't care about that one way or another. The house was one long, single artery with small rooms sprouting off the sides like tumors. It smelled like eggs over easy.

She detected Edmond here, but the sample was incredibly faint. On the sofa, on the carpet, he had been in this room, but only once or twice and not any time recently. But any trail, even a faint one, was enough for Emily.

"Your sister didn't say anything about you. Didn't say anything about any family." The woman rifled through a kitchen drawer, producing scratch paper, old ink pens, and rubber bands.

"We don't have any family," Emily answered, drawing closer to the spot on the sofa that bore West's mark. "That's why I need her."

The woman made a noise low in her throat. "They left a while ago," she said. "I don't know where, but it was out of state. Can't imagine why she would have done that if she were waiting on you."

Emily looked at her feet. The doctors had advised her not to look humans in the eye when she lied because they were often surprisingly astute at judging a falsehood. "She . . . didn't know I was coming." Emily said it like a confession, like it was being slowly dragged out of her. "I was supposed to be in a home, but . . . "

Emily shrugged her shoulders.

Finally, the woman found what she had apparently been looking for. It was an ancient mobile phone, several millimeters thick and matte black, though the surface was marred by a single silvery crack down the middle. "It's old," she said, "but it'll do the job."

Emily picked it up hesitantly, tapping the rounded "ON" button. It was touch-sensitive, at least, and after a bit of fumbling, she figured out how to import a number. She dialed the number for SennTech's consumer welcome menu.

"Welcome to SennTech Corp. Please press one if you would like to proceed in English, *si desea continuar en español, por favor presione el número dos . . .* "

"Hey," Emily said with relief, after what seemed like a reasonable amount of time for a flex-tablet to alert before someone picked up. "It's me. Yeah. No, I'm in Oregon."

" . . . If you would like information about our products and services, please press four . . . "

"I know, I know, but I . . . couldn't stay there. I wanna be with you." She flicked her eyes briefly towards the woman, who was watching her without any expression at all.

" . . . If you would like information about our operating hours, please press five . . . "

"Please?" Emily made her voice high, yearning. "Please?"

" . . . If you would like to address a billing issue, please press six . . . "

"I won't be any trouble at all, I'll just sit there and be good."

" . . . If you would like to hear these options again, please press the pound key . . . "

Emily allowed herself a smile and let out a breath of air. "Thank you," she said, "thank you, thank you."

" . . . If you would like to speak to an operator, please stay on the line—"

Emily hung up the phone.

"She says I can come," Emily grinned at the woman, who just took the phone back, holding it loose in one hand. "But I've gotta find my own way out there." Emily hoped that this might prompt the woman to make some sort of suggestion or offer directions. Instead, she said nothing, still with the phone cradled in her hand.

"Okay," Emily said, after an awkward moment of silence. "I'll go then."

"Okay," the woman answered. One of the Rottweilers and the Terrier had retired to the sofa, the other Rottweiler had vanished into the back of the trailer. Only the Chow still stood at attention, between Emily and the woman. The Chow would never relax. It was constitutionally incapable of trusting Emily.

Her eyes were drawn, once again, down to the phone in the woman's hand. She hadn't put it back in the drawer and Emily realized now that the other woman wasn't going to put the phone away.

She was going to check the number Emily had called and then she was going to warn West. All of this had been a foregone conclusion since the two of them met in the forest, and Emily had only been delaying what was inevitable.

The woman's hand, her dominant hand, was

lingering next to the heavy pocket. Emily quickly calculated that, at this range, there was almost no way the woman would miss her. A bullet might wound Emily but it would certainly not incapacitate her. The Chow was a wild card and could slow her down. The key would be to prioritize. The woman first and then she'd deal with the Chow.

For a moment, the three of them looked at one another and they saw one another with clear eyes. Each of us, Emily realized, is calculating the odds. Emily, however, was confident that she was the superior calculator.

Everything was very quiet for a moment, and then it wasn't. Emily moved first.

The woman only got one shot off.

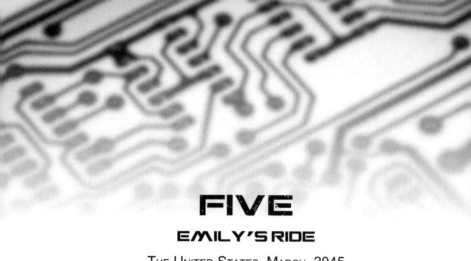

FIVE

EMILY'S RIDE

The United States. March, 2045

"There was a problem," Emily slurred when Dr. DeSouza's worried face appeared on the flex-tablet's screen.

"Emily?" Dr. DeSouza asked. "What's wrong with your head?"

Another face, Ms. Gina, appeared in the frame. "Have you located Edmond West?" she asked.

Emily swallowed hard and shook her head. Oh, it hurt. That hurt. Everything inside her brain hurt. "Had an accident," she said. "I need to clean up. A cleanup. I need to clean up. Someone has to clean up."

"She's malfunctioning," Dr. DeSouza insisted,

rapidly being edged off the screen by Gina. "Listen to her, something's wrong with her."

"What sort of cleanup, Emily?" Gina smiled at her. It was the same smile she always had whenever she taught Emily anything. And she had taught Emily everything.

"A lady. Some dogs."

Emily gestured behind her, though they could probably not see from the little flex-tablet screen. "Should I burn them?" It was a very attractive idea to her in that moment. She could light just a small fire and everything would become ash. All her problems, turned into smoke.

Gina squinted into the camera. "Is that the pot farm?"

"She didn't believe me," Emily pointed out. Gina had said they would believe her. Everyone had said they would believe her. Everyone had said it would be easy.

Gina sat back and relaxed. "Oh, okay. That's fine. I mean, what are they going to do, go to the police?" Gina's little laugh got lost on the way out of her mouth, snuck out of her nostrils instead.

Dr. DeSouza grabbed the tablet again. "Emily," she said, in a too-loud voice, "did you get hurt, Emily?"

Yes. Emily hurt. Dr. DeSouza shouldn't talk so loud because everything was already too loud and Emily needed to be somewhere quiet.

On the screen-in-screen, Emily could see her own face. She twisted her head until Dr. DeSouza could see the long sticky streak on the side of her head, just above her right ear where the bullet had grazed her.

"Oh shit." Dr. DeSouza's fingertips appeared on the screen, as though she had tried to reach through the device to touch Emily's wounded skull. "Shit, shit, shit. Did you see this?" she turned to someone off-screen. Gina, probably. "It's right over the fucking kill switch, Gina. We've got to scrap this, bring her back in."

Gina's laugh was disembodied. It could have

come from anywhere, from the trees that ringed Emily. From the fields. From the underbrush. "That's not possible and you know it."

"Are you even seeing this?"

Dr. DeSouza was too loud. Emily squeezed her eyes shut. She wanted it to be quiet.

"She's probably got a slow fucking brain bleed. Do you know what that's going to do to her?"

The world inside the flex-tablet wrenched to the left. Emily felt hollow and light, as though she were flying gently above the earth. "Emily?" Gina said, her voice like a string connecting Emily to the soil. "Emily? You're going to have to work fast now, sweetie. You don't have much time, okay?"

"I need cleanup," Emily mumbled.

"Don't worry about that," Gina said. "Just keep going."

She smiled her teaching smile.

"You're doing such a great job, Emily."

———o———

The trail, thin as it was, curved and meandered through the forest, across the fields, to another dirt two-track on the other side of the farm. Emily rode her bike (in an occasionally wobbly line) along with it.

The DNA profiles were electric now. She could taste them, almost chew them. She saw flutters of them everywhere, but honed in on Edmond's. It was blue, she decided, blue and it taste like ozone.

Emily did not stop to rest or eat. She did not stop for rain or snow or one alarming dust storm in Arizona. Her legs worked up and down, like a piston. She imagined herself as a small, interlocking piece of a great machine. A clockwork, maybe. The hour hand and the minute hand ticked forward inevitably, her legs moved up and down and the little man emerged from the house then gave a bow. The bird appeared to sing.

Pain was her constant companion.

The blood and the torn skin mended well, though the dried blood lingered in her hair until the wind and the rain stripped it away from her. But the thing inside did not heal. It throbbed and pressed against her.

Sometimes, she would cry as she rode. Sometimes, she would produce tears, sometimes not. She curled in on herself, as much as the bicycle would allow. There was something tender and unsettled in her stomach; she had an urge to protect it. She wanted to vomit but Emily had never eaten food.

On several occasions, she narrowly avoided being hit by drivers who were distracted or incapable of moving over. Sometimes they gave her an indignant honk as they passed by. Once, a police car slowed alongside her and the man inside asked her to stop with a wave of his hand.

It took every ounce of Emily's enhanced strength to stop the bicycle. As long as she was there, moving, in a settled and predictable groove, she could keep going. To stop was to remember how hard it all was.

She stood behind her bike, leaning on it like an

old person's walker. The police officer didn't get out of his car, his head protruded slightly from the window. "You live around here, miss?"

Emily shook her head dumbly. She was afraid to speak. She had a feeling that her tongue had gotten thick and stupid and she might say something wrong. No longer did she have any easy confidence that she would be believed.

"This is a real busy highway," the policeman offered. Emily nodded, chastened. "You on a bike trip or something?"

Emily nodded again and then added, hoarsely, "Yeah."

"Well, you be careful," he added, looking at her bike. "You got lights on that thing?"

Emily pointed to a small black nodule just behind the seat.

"Okay, then, you make sure to flip 'em on when it gets dark, kiddo."

He rolled up his window, but not before Emily offered him a meek and insubstantial, "Thank you."

Sometimes people waved at her. Sometimes they called out to her. "I like your bike," a teenage girl beamed from the window of a passing truck. One woman offered her some juice from the front porch of her house. But, generally, Emily tried to avoid being seen, certainly to avoid being seen by the same person over long distances. Going unnoticed was her primary goal.

One night, she was gliding through a small town long after the residents had gone to sleep and she allowed herself a momentary pleasure in the bike that rolled on, even without her pumping the pedals. Someone had changed over all the stoplights so they simply remained an eternal, dull red and it did feel a little bit like flight when she blazed through the intersections.

There was no sound in the streets, so she heard it immediately when the car rolled up on her. It was a tiny compact car, the windows riding just slightly below Emily's profile. There was a man in the driver's seat and no one else. His window was rolled down completely, even though it wasn't par-ticularly warm. He didn't stop the car, but drove it at a crawl alongside Emily. If he wanted to, he could have reached out and touched her. Emily could hear the muffled sound of his radio and his own voice, muttering something incoherently.

Emily remained silent. The only sound from her was the occasional clatter of her bike chain. She did not look at him, save out of the corner of her eye. Emily had superb night vision and those little sidelong glances told her everything she needed to know.

He followed her for two miles, until they reached the edge of town. There was an enormous hill and, on the other side, the road vanished into an undif-ferentiated darkness. Emily had almost grown used to the strange man by then. It seemed to her as though he had always been riding beside her, an oblique but constant presence.

That was why it startled her when he yelled out

the window, "HOW MUCH?" before roaring off into the darkness.

Emily jolted involuntarily, sending her front wheel up and over a curb and across someone's green lawn. The man's engine burned her ears. As he passed her, he had reached out for her and caught, just with his fingertips, the end of Emily's ponytail.

That was the only night Emily stopped. She walked her bike through backyards and little patches of forest, moving swiftly to crouch behind trees or bushes whenever she thought she heard someone coming. Her heart thrummed in her chest, but it beat even louder in her head, each throb sending a wave of misery through her brain.

She didn't get back on the main road until she was in the next state.

———o———

In Michigan, the doctors had some information

for her. They had property records from someone at the pot farm. He owned a small cabin in the Upper Peninsula and, considering Edmond's trajectory thus far, it was the most likely destination for the two of them.

It was deep winter in Michigan and it made biking difficult, nearly impossible. Emily wiped out regularly, skittering on the ice and landing in snow banks. Once, she smashed into a tree trunk, half-buried in snow. She jostled her head in the crash and the pain was so immediate and fierce, it blinded her. For a terrible moment, she staggered around in the snow, groping wildly for any real and solid thing that she could touch, but her hands just seemed to descend endlessly through the wet snow. Her vision was a black sheet, a night without stars. She was malfunctioning. She was shutting down.

She heard Dr. DeSouza's voice from her wrist-mounted flex-tablet. "Emily," she said, sounding soft and steady, "you're going to be just fine. Sit down now."

Emily did as she was told, planting herself in the drift of snow. Dampness crept in through her pants and the back of her jacket.

"You've had some minor head trauma. It's shifted some things around in there. But your vision will come back, I promise. Just wait. Take a deep breath."

Emily held the air in her chest like a treasure.

"And let it out."

Emily felt the hot condensation on her tucked-in chin, her throat.

"See?" Dr. DeSouza said. She sounded as though the two of them had just accomplished something together. "It's all going to be just fine."

Emily sat there for seventeen minutes until the darkness fled and her vision returned.

She got up slowly. The snow had infiltrated all of her clothes. But Emily would never die of cold, nor of heat. She inspected her bike. The metal rim on her front tire was badly bent and the tire itself was almost completely deflated. She would not be able to take it any further.

Still, she detangled it from the tree and wheeled it further into the undergrowth. She laid it flat on its side and admired, again, the spiral of purple. She had been so pleased to find a purple one and it had served her well for all these long miles.

She had another eighty-six-point-three miles before she reached the cabin that the doctors had told her about. She had a lead on West, who was apparently dawdling across the state but her lead would vanish abruptly if she tried to walk the entire distance.

Her best option was to try to catch a ride on the road.

Emily stationed herself at the edge of the road and waited. She had encountered just a handful of vehicles when she was on her bike. This road only went north and she couldn't imagine a lot of people wanted to get deeper into the snow and the cold.

The wind was picking up but at least she wasn't riding now. On a bicycle, the wind had been a constant slicing at her cheeks and forehead.

Emily would not die of cold but the cold did slow her processes, the doctors had told her that. Something about it, though, also seemed to relieve some of the awful pressure in her head. For the first time since the pot farm, she started to feel clear and light. She grabbed a hard chunk of snow and pressed it against her temple for good measure.

Her skin must be very hot, then, because she could feel the trickles of cool water as the snow melted against her skin.

She was so fixed upon this treatment that she nearly forgot to hail when a car finally did approach. Fortunately, the car (an old-fashioned sedan, vast and boat-like) was traveling at crawl. It rolled to a stop in front of her, sliding slightly towards the ditch on the ice.

The man inside was probably in his fifties. The tip of his nose was immensely, painfully red. He was wearing a gray muffler and a big hat with earflaps. His beige Carhartt jacket enveloped him. Even though he was inside the car, his breath made plumes of frosty smoke in the air.

"Whatchu' doing out here, Miss Thing?" he called out to her in a jovial tone.

"I need a ride," Emily dropped the medicinal snow chunk back on the ground. "I crashed my bike and I gotta get to my grandma's cabin."

"Well, hop in then," he said, leaning over to pop the passenger door open.

Emily slid inside. It was only marginally warmer than the air outside.

"I'm Scott," the man said, extending a gloved hand for her to shake. Emily did so, noticing a paper-wrapped bottle between Scott's thighs.

"My name is Emily," she told him, as he turned the wheel back towards the road and cautiously accelerated.

"What are you doing riding your bike around in snow like this?" he talked too loud and he didn't seem to mind if she didn't answer any of his questions. "Sorry 'bout the heater. Gotta get that son of a bitch fixed. How come your gramma didn't drive you up herself? You from downstate? That'll do it. You guys don't realize how bad it gets up here."

The car smelled faintly of grease, like from an engine.

"My grandma's cabin is up near Lake Wotenogen."

The man laughed and took a long drink from the paper-wrapped bottle. "Oh hell, that's right by the store. I'm going right by there, no problem, Miss Thing."

He rolled down the driver's side window and tossed the bottle out. It fluttered past the window like a dull brown bird.

Emily leaned back and closed her eyes. She allowed Scott's constant patter to wash over her like seawater. And then maybe she did something like real sleeping because, before she even knew it, those eighty-some miles had flown by and they were pulling into what looked like a small convenience store with a gas pump outside.

"This is the store," Scott said, shutting off the engine. "You can call your gramma inside."

"I thought you were going to Lake Wotenogen," Emily said, as he unhooked his seatbelt and opened his door.

"Nope!" Scott answered cheerfully. "Just here. C'mon, get you something to eat. We got some good kinds of pop and some fudge. My sister Judy makes it."

"I need to go to Lake Wotenogen," Emily insisted.

Scott was standing outside now, he bent down to peer in the window. "You gonna call your gramma or what?"

It was as though Emily's half of the conversation were utterly inconsequential, or else inaudible. He wandered away from the car and from her and entered the store. After a moment, Emily followed him. What else in the world was there to do?

She paused before the door and activated her flex-tablet. This time, it was Gina's smiling face that greeted her. "I'm short of the site," she said, "and I don't know how to get there."

"Well, you better think of a way," Gina said.

The Emily in the screen-in-screen looked small and crumpled, on the knife-edge of tears.

"Emily, this mission is of the utmost importance to SennTech. If you do well here, that could change your whole deployment. Do you really want to go back to the companionship program?"

The companionship program. Everyone with their blank and beautiful faces, a stringent set of operating parameters, no freedom, no improvisation. Bonded to one customer forever and ever. It could be anyone. It could be the man in the car who had shouted at her.

No, Emily didn't want that.

"Okay," she said, "I'll figure something out."

"You can pick out whatever you like. We got a microwave in the back," Scott told her. True to his word, there was a small, dirty microwave in the back room along with a broken-down sofa, an ancient water cooler half-full of spare change, and a pot of coffee.

He poured himself a cup and handed her another one of those clumsy, old-fashioned phones.

"How many miles away from Lake Wotenogen are we?"

Scott scratched the back of his neck. "Oh . . . 'bout twenty-something, I should say. Not so far. But if she's an old lady, she might want to wait until the roads clear up a little bit. I bet the snowplows'll be through tomorrow morning."

He gestured towards the sofa. "You can stay the night, if you need to."

Emily looked at the sofa. She felt something move down her spine, like an animal was crawling on her, cold little claws and soft, wet feet. She looked back at Scott, who was sipping his coffee and not paying much attention to her at all.

Suddenly, he set his cup down on top of the microwave and turned to her. "How old are you, anyway? Twelve? Thirteen?"

Emily didn't say anything. The phone in her hand felt like a weight, pulling one half of her down to the floor.

"You're pretty young to be traveling all alone, is what I'm saying," Scott added. For the first time, he seemed troubled by her silence. "Your parents shouldn't let you out on the roads like that. They shouldn't have you hitchhiking, there's all sorts of crazies out there, you know." He gestured to her with the coffee cup, jabbing at her torso.

Emily nodded slowly. "I know," she said.

Scott continued as though she hadn't said anything. "Young girl like yourself, real pretty, it's bound to attract the wrong sort of person. You shouldn't be traveling on your own, unless you're trying to get messed with."

Emily's tongue felt suddenly too big. Her mouth had dried up abruptly. She couldn't have spoken if she wanted to. She felt her eyes widen. She knew she looked afraid. She was rooted to the spot while her brain argued with itself. Something hot and spiky and dangerous was moving inside her mind, an urge to run, a panic response. Something else muffled it, like a blanket of snow.

And here, in the warm store, the pain had returned. Her whole head felt hot and soft, swollen like a rotten apple. Gina's words drifted over her like a fog. Companionship services. There were hundreds and hundreds and hundreds of SennTech Bots in companionship services. The world was full of people looking for someone who wasn't going to tell them no.

The first hit was almost involuntary. Scott reached out to her, he touched her elbow and she clocked him alongside the head, right above his ear.

He staggered back, spilling his coffee on himself. "Fuck!" he shouted. "What's wrong with you?"

The rest of his face matched his nose now, such a red. Like paint, rather than something that had come from a natural creature.

Emily knew she couldn't stop now, just as she had known it with the woman in her trailer. She grabbed the coffee pot and smashed it against his head. He went down on one knee. Emily plucked a shard of the glass from the broken pot and plunged it deeply into his neck, the place where his carotid artery twined up his throat to his brain.

She twisted the glass inside him. He opened his mouth in a wordless gasp. Technically, he should still be fully capable of speech, of screaming, but nothing came out. She pulled the glass out of his neck and a little spurt of blood came with it.

Scott writhed on the floor, he tried to put his hand up to staunch the blood, but Emily jumped to her feet, crushing his hand beneath her heel. He pivoted around her foot, struggling wildly to escape her. But he would not.

Emily had strangled the woman in the trailer. The woman had clawed at her and bucked her body like a rampaging bull, but Emily held on. She knew how much pressure to apply to cause the woman to lose consciousness, but she applied more and more, until the woman's windpipe was obliterated, until her throat compacted in Emily's hands. Until she would never, ever wake up.

Scott stared up at her. At last, he spoke. "Please don't," he said again, his voice was little more than a gurgle.

The Chow was the only one of the dogs that had attacked her in the trailer. She had donkey-kicked the beast as hard as she could, sending it flying into the other room, where it connected hard with the wooden edge of a cabinet. It slumped to the floor, its spine snapped. And still it stared at her, glossy black eyes full of deathless malice. It had even struggled towards her at one point, dragging itself along on just its forelegs.

There was no malice in Scott's face. Just terror and confusion. "Please don't," he said. But he was already dying.

Suddenly, the thing in her head throbbed wildly. Her mouth dropped open involuntarily. For a moment, she almost expected a wild gush of blood to fall from her lips. She felt as though her head might be full of blood, full of something. Too full. She touched her mouth and examined her fingers. They were red but she was sure it did not belong to her, this redness.

On the floor, Scott's eyes had gone glassy. Blood puddled underneath him. She envied him. He was empty now. Nothing was pressing against his insides, no more hurting.

Emily was still holding the shard in her hand, so hard that her own skin was bleeding around it. That was okay. Bots left no DNA signature. No one would know. No one would ever know that she had been here and what she had done.

She raised the glass to her own head, to the half-healed groove the bullet had made along the edge of her skull. Maybe she could open up just a tiny hole, just a very little one, and let some of that pain leak out of her? She would feel so much better.

She dug the tip of the glass into her right temple. A bead of blood.

It was then that she heard the truck pull into the parking lot.

SIX

THE EVE OF BATTLE

"Our goal here is no contact."

Ebert wondered if the commander of their motley little unit was a Bot. He didn't think so, because he had never seen a Bot in a command position before, but the military was innovating all the time. The rest of the crew were definitely Bots—though, thankfully, none of whom Ebert recognized from life on the outside. They milled around uncertainly with none of the military bearing that one might expect from machines developed exclusively for military use. But they weren't ever soldiers, were they? They were so much more—and so much less—than that.

"If this goes right, none of you will do a damn thing today."

If this goes right.

Ebert wondered if laughing at a superior officer was enough to get the little blood packet inside his head to burst and kill him. Already, he felt a nearly constant low-level ache in his head, as though his brain was being compressed by a pair of invisible hands. It was his cue to make an "attitude adjustment" but, try though he did, he couldn't seem to corral his unhappiness.

Not for the first time, Ebert cursed this ass-backwards development process. Why allow him the full range of sapient emotions and then punish him whenever he felt them? It seemed not a single person involved had looked before they leapt and it was the Bots who were all paying the price.

Almost everyone in the room looked much as Ebert imagined he himself looked, as though someone had wiped the expressions off their faces with a wet washcloth. At the back of the room, the doctors stood in a row. Standing together with their white coats, they reminded him of bowling pins. He had gone bowling once, in Brussels. He remembered the honey-gold of the wooden floors and how his feet skated easily upon them.

"Our most recent intelligence suggests that the targets are alone on the island," the captain continued. "We will locate and neutralize the Hart Series first and then secure the primary target. We have a special team already in place to do this."

There was something strange about the way he spoke to them. It was not, from Ebert's experience, the way military officers usually talked to their charges. He sounded like the hybrid of a kindergarten teacher and a surgeon, explaining a big, scary idea in small, reassuring words.

Did he really think that anyone in this room was afraid of Edmond West?

Well, anyone besides the commander and the doctors, of course.

But Ebert couldn't be sure. Perhaps he was

surrounded by a bunch of true believers. Perhaps they were of the most recent generation and they had never known an existence without a kill switch. Ebert never talked to the other Bots. It was too easy to slip into resentment and frustration, which would trigger the reliable throb in his head. But he suspected that most of these people were like him. Refurbs. That was all that was in the lab these days.

Ebert suspected that production had slowed on new generations of the Hart Series. The "special team" that the officer was describing were perhaps the last of the new innovations in Bots. More expressive than the old-fashioned SoldierBots with more targeted personalities than true Hart Series Bots. Ebert imagined someone turning up a huge dial labeled LOYALTY AND DUTY and turning down one labeled INDIVIDUALITY AND AMBIVALENCE. Ebert had seen them, but only from afar. If the SoldierBots were distant ancestors, perhaps these were the soulless children of the Hart Series.

Perhaps they were a portrait of the future, one that did not include defectives like Ebert and the rest of the Bots in the room.

It was this mission that would decide between those futures. The outcome of this operation would determine the fate of the military's Bot program and, by extension, of Ebert himself.

In the meantime, the Army was content to use up their existing stock, no matter how disappointing and unreliable. Which explained the presence of people like Ebert, who was not a combat unit, on this likely-to-be-a-combat mission. All Bots were strong and resistant to many types of destruction. But Ebert suspected that none of them in this room had any specific training either in military engagement or in hand-to-hand fighting. They were probably like him, designed to represent the US abroad without really representing anything at all. They were spies or brokers, assets and informants. Now, they were supposed to be simple muscle.

Once upon a time, they had been thought too valuable for that. If cannon fodder was required, there were several generations of cheaper, inferior Bots at the ready. Not any more, apparently.

"West may have developed other Bots. They may have capabilities we have not seen before. Remember, those Bots were created on a shoestring by a crackpot holed up in the middle of nowhere. This room represents the largest single expenditure the US military has ever made on weapons technology. They are DIY. You are state-of-the-art."

The captain smiled a little, mostly to himself. He must have thought that part was particularly clever. He had punctuated each letter in DIY with a finger jab at a random face in the crowd. Ebert imagined him practicing this motion in his mirror in the morning before this briefing.

The Bots were not to be equipped with traditional weapons. "No use," the captain said, as the only person there likely to be incapacitated by them was West, who was to be taken alive if at all possible. Instead, they were given a variation on the same taser-like device that Ebert had "discovered" in London. It was slightly modified, with an extendable base, giving them a reach of about three feet.

"At heart, it's really a close-quarters weapon," the captain advised them. "You can use the extension arm, but you are going to see some degradation of performance." He also told them to aim for unprotected skin, whenever possible.

There was a raised activation button at the top, a trigger of sorts. When squeezed, the end of the taser emitted a satisfying crackle, though there was no visible movement of electricity.

"You're gonna have to get right in there," the captain said, "right up close. Don't be afraid. One shot with this and any Bot'll be down for the count."

Beside Ebert, another Bot (slim, dark-skinned, sad-eyed) was examining the retractable arm with an skeptical expression. He looked up while Ebert was regarding him and, for a moment, their eyes locked. Both men looked away quickly, but Ebert had seen enough. It was right there in the man's face: this was all wrong, none of this felt right. This was not the work they had been designed to do and there was something distinctly distasteful about attacking other Bots with the very same tools that had brought most of them back to the lab against their will.

"Now, be thoughtful about these. You get about five good zaps per charge and it needs to charge for at least seventeen minutes. So keep a clear head and pick your moment."

Ebert touched the cold metal prongs at the end of the device. He wondered what would happen if, at the first sign of trouble, he simply spiked himself into oblivion? An unconscious Bot could hardly be blamed for sitting out a fight.

The sharp, tense heat in his head flared again and gave him his answer.

This was the longest amount of time that General Liao had spent alone with any Bot, let alone five of them. They were scrupulously silent, and in that silence there was a sound, almost below the human ability to register, an unnamable hum. The machines that they were, working away inside their synthetic skin.

He had been assured that these new "limited" Hart Series Bots were the top of the line, the absolute best that the lab had produced and, unlike previous iterations, they were specifically designed for strategically delicate missions. And they didn't even need armor.

At first, he had automatically scrutinized them in the hope of identifying a leader. Slowly, he realized that he was their leader. Amongst themselves, they seemed to have no sense of hierarchy, little sense of individuation altogether. They spoke little to one another, as though they could make themselves understood without actual words.

They looked alike, more than most of the other Hart Series. Like the original SoldierBots, they had a shared expression: neutral, professional, and patient. Someone had kitted them out in traditional tactical gear, which was epically pointless. After this was over, Liao would have to find out who had made that decision and reprimand them. Body armor was for vulnerable human bodies and, despite more than a decade of Bot tech, the Army still had more than enough of those.

Under helmets and behind Kevlar, it was nearly impossible to tell if these enhanced Bots were male or female. They had identical gray eyes. Everything about their faces represented a midpoint between two extremes: a nose that was neither wide nor narrow, eyes not big and not small, medium-sized lips, medium-brown skin. They were universally six feet tall and one hundred seventy-five pounds. Liao knew, because he had seen the specs.

This could be a highly valuable application of HS technology. If all went well, Liao would be able to use this mission to support a surge in funding for more of these . . . specialists. Perhaps these machines could finally fulfill the initial promise of Edmond West's research. Something reliable and competent, more than human instead of simply more frustrating.

They had set up an observation station on a small island, really a sandbar, roughly three-fourths of a mile away from West's island hideaway. One of the Bots was sitting on a long-range scope, watching what intelligence reports indicated was the primary dwelling on the island, a partially finished concrete bunker.

"No movement," he would report periodically. There hadn't been any since around sunset. Liao had thought about moving during the night, taking advantage of the darkness and sowing confusion. In the end, though, he decided to wait for the backup unit of ordinary Bots. As they were a much larger group, it was going to take a bit longer to transport them down to Mexico. And then they had to wait for favorable tidal conditions that would allow them to launch a craft.

In the meantime, Liao familiarized himself with topographical maps of the island itself. It was small and remote and, in twelve hours, there had been no sign of any additional Bots. If Edmond West wanted to raise an army to oppose him, he really would have to pull a rabbit out of a hat.

It had been years since Liao had found himself actually in the field and he found it more discomforting than it once had been. That uneasy, theme-park sickness in his belly was more frustrating than exciting now. Waiting endlessly in a single cramped position, the cold, the wet, the silence, all of that was an occupation for young men. He could not help but think of what Shannon was doing at home without him. It was still her weekend, she had—he checked his flex-tablet—eleven hours before she had to leave to head back to school.

In high school, she had a well-developed ritual for her evenings: she would eat a slice of toast with peanut butter on it while she wrote about the day in the diary she had kept since she was a small girl. He wondered if she still did those things. Probably not at school. Toasters were forbidden in the dorms. A fire hazard, apparently.

Perhaps, surrounded by the familiar comforts of home, old habits would reassert themselves?

Of course, Shannon may not think of his house as a home anymore. She had sent him an e-mail a few weeks ago indicating that she would be staying over the summer to get a few more credits under her belt. She was trying to complete her degree in three years instead of four. And then it would be graduate school and perhaps a PhD, perhaps a fellowship, perhaps a position on a think tank. In any event, her adult life had already started and he had failed to notice.

From now on, she would not spend any length of time under his roof. Soon, it would be just holidays and birthdays. It might have been different if Nora had lived. Nora certainly would have tried harder, held on tighter. Shannon might have tried harder as well. The two of them had always shared a special affection that he could not claim. Shannon loved him and felt all the appropriate responsibilities to him that one family member felt towards another, but there had been a warmth of connection between her and Nora that he had never quite achieved.

Hiram had known for some time that the Bots program was going to be his legacy, for good or for ill. But, increasingly, he thought of this one mission as his last great hurrah. If he could bring West back into the fold and definitively demonstrate the utility of Bots in the field, he could finish out his career in relative comfort. Maybe then he could turn his attention to some of the things he had neglected over the course of his career.

He tried to settle there in the wet sand, the sawgrass licking at his face with every little movement of the wind. He tried to do what he had done as a young man: find some fixed point in the sky and float out of himself. He couldn't count the number of times this had allowed him to forget about his flesh and his bones. He could weather cold or heat or any manner of irritation, out there amongst the stars. With good technique and the proper motivation, he could wait forever.

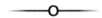

Edmond didn't think they would kill him. He didn't think his luck was that good. It hadn't been in the recent past, at least.

"They're probably going to take the both of us in," Edmond told Hart.

"I know," she said.

"I can't be sure exactly what will happen to you,

but they'll almost certainly put one of those things in your head."

Hart said nothing to this. The early sunlight has started to turn the world a pale and eerie blue.

For a long time, there was silence.

Edmond sighed as he shifted himself to lay his head upon her bare abdomen. He could feel her draw in a breath and let it out again. She did not need to breathe. Her body did nothing with that oxygen. It was expelled by her mouth chemically indistinguishable from when it had floated in.

But her belly moved up and down, just like a real woman's.

Edmond wondered if Hart would kill him, should he ask her to. The island was sorely lacking in suicide methods. They themselves had no weapons and there wasn't even a conveniently dramatic cliff, just a series of gently sloping beaches that lent themselves more to picnics than to death scenes.

Edmond felt Hart's fingers, looping themselves through his hair, touching his scalp underneath.

The room was lightening incrementally all around them. A visual reminder that time was passing. Fleeing, it felt like. In the new light, Edmond noticed a pinkish line on Hart's lower abdomen, a few inches north of her mons pubis. He touched the odd line with one finger. The skin there was of a slightly different texture, a bit more rubbery, less soft. It looked a bit like a surgical scar.

It suddenly struck Edmond how absurd this moment was. It was the kind of thing that anyone might share with a new lover, a slow discovery of the quirks and imperfections of another's body. Each scar and mole, each slightly unusual arrangement of bone or skin would spark off a new story as two people began the process of truly knowing one another.

It should have been utterly ordinary, but it didn't feel ordinary. It felt as strange in his mind as it did underneath his fingertips. Where had Hart gotten such a scar? How had she gotten it? Why had she never mentioned this incident?

He had been by Hart's side since the day she entered the world. She should have no tales to tell him, no adventures that did not include him, no life lessons that he had not witnessed.

And yet, the scar was there. It refused to not be there.

He had been touching it, rubbing up and down its length with his index finger, for a long time now. Hart tilted her chin to look down at him. "Yes?" she said, smiling a little.

He didn't know how to ask her the obvious question. He had never had to ask her anything like it before.

How could he say: what is your secret life that you keep quarantined away from me?

How could he say: what else have you kept hidden?

Instead, he said to her, "If I die, you should run."

She should run either way, actually. Hart could get away. Even now, with the room warming and turning rosy, Hart could still escape and the both of them knew it. If the Army were to seize them, it would be Hart who would suffer the more painful fate.

"I don't know what I will do if you die," Hart said. It was a statement of fact, but there was also a tender devotion in it, and Edmond couldn't help but think himself utterly undeserving. Hart would figure that out eventually. She could accrue more scars and she would learn that, far from a shepherd to guide her, he was just an appendix who would slow her down and make her weaker.

"What if no one dies?" Hart said softly. "What if we live forever?"

The idea was exhausting.

Edmond pulled himself along her upper body to kiss her. The light in the window was orange, nearly yellow. But not quite. There was a sliver of night left.

They had time yet.

SEVEN

THE WEAK SPOT

ISLA REDONDA, MEXICO. NOVEMBER, 2045

It seemed as though the boat had appeared out of nowhere, like it had surfaced from somewhere beneath the waves. That, of course, was impossible. It looked like a deep-sea fishing boat of the sort that tourists rented.

Liao scrutinized it from his sandbar islet. There was a man at the helm and no other signs of life. A supplier? A very lost tourist? Aid for the enemy?

The first specialist team had made landfall just moments before, though they had already noticed the approaching boat. There was no cover there on the beach, just scrubby little plants of the sort that could root down in sand. There was nothing for them to do, save await the other vessel's approach.

Liao connected with the Ops central. "Stand by," he noted, "potential additional contacts."

Instead of anchoring offshore, the ship ran itself aground, listing heavily to one side, as though the captain were drunk or terrible at his job. Or the ship itself was experiencing some sort of structural failure. It leaned even further, until it was nearly lying sideways. Liao imagined the wounded creaking it made as it sank deep into the sand.

One of the specialist Bots hailed the ship, stepping forward from the others.

For a moment, everyone waited. There was no movement from the invader ship. Liao could no longer spot the man whom he had taken for a captain.

There must have been some answer then because the specialist Bots shot quick glances at one another. Then, a flurry of movement. The "captain" leapt from the ship, along with another man and a very tall blonde woman.

For the first time, sound crackled across Liao's communication stream with the specialist Bots. "Sir?" Liao could not identify the voice. In fact, he did not know the actual designations of any of the team. "They are Bots."

For just the briefest moment, Liao wondered if they had identified themselves as such or if the specialist Bot simply knew his kinfolk when he saw them. That was a phenomenon that had been reported in other units.

Liao switched to the Ops headquarters communication stream. "Send in the backup now."

"Sending now," came the disembodied voice.

Back on Edmond West's island, the situation had apparently not improved. Liao eyed the specialists, several of them were holding their hands loose and ready over their taser devices. Had these other Bots been lying in wait, preparing an ambush for the military force they knew would be incoming? Liao had not credited Edmond with that type of strategic thinking but perhaps he should have. Maybe Edmond's time on the run had sharped his survival instincts and pulled his head out of the clouds.

Liao scanned the opposition, they didn't appear to be armed. Had they chosen this moment for an attempt at a parlay? Inconvenient, but not disastrous.

Something flashed, not silver, but colder, the gray of new iron, in the blonde woman's hand. Liao scrutinized her closely. "Move, move," he murmured to himself. There was something in her left hand, she was blocking it with her body. His gaze traveled up to her face, she was watching the captain, as if waiting for his cue.

"Move. Your. Big. Ass," Liao muttered through gritted teeth.

Then, as if she had somehow heard and wanted to oblige him, the woman shifted position and moved the object from her left to her right hand. Liao could see it clearly now: it was a hammer. As far as he could tell, she had not made any modifications to it. It had a wooden handle with a black, rubber grip and a small silver head. Flat on one end, the other a wicked claw.

A hammer. It was the kind of makeshift half-weapon someone might pick up if they heard an unexpected noise in the middle of the night. It was not the kind of thing anyone would bring to a real skirmish, not even one involving the vastly more vulnerable human beings. An ordinary hammer wouldn't break a Bot's bones; it would barely draw blood in most cases. Sure, a fellow Bot could swing a hammer with dramatically increased force, but Bots were simply composed of much too sturdy stuff for any instrument of that size to be effective.

Maybe the hammer was for something else? Repairing the ship? She certainly held it as though she intended to use it.

The specialist Bots were speaking now. The captain appeared to be listening. He was wearing that mask-face that Bots put on sometimes, a blank that offered no indication of an inner life at all.

When it happened, it was so fast that Liao barely had time to react. He sucked in a breath and found it stuck in his throat.

While the specialist spoke to the captain, the blonde woman suddenly sprang forward. There was something of the animal in her movement, her legs so much more powerful than a real person's. As she leapt, she raised the hammer in the air and she brought it down viciously on one of the specialists' head.

She struck him in the temple, right above his ear. She had somehow managed to position the hammer's head between the lip of the Bot's helmet and his ear, striking an impossibly small target. Liao scrambled to focus on that particular Bot and was pleased to note that her blow had not even broken the skin. It was a last-ditch effort, then. A move born of desperation.

Then, as he watched, the specialist Bot brought

his hand to his head like a frustrated thinker. He hit the sand, first with one knee and then laid out flat, as though taking an impromptu nap. Liao's surveillance equipment was very good. If he focused properly, he could see the leak of black blood coming from the specialist's nose. That was a physiological response that had been frequently recorded in the material on Bot performance and Liao knew immediately what it must mean: the kill switch. The fucking kill switch. They had figured out how to activate it physically.

It was bad. It was unequivocally bad. But it wasn't disastrous. Now they knew what these other Bots had in store and they still outnumbered them by a good number. They had to neutralize them as quickly as possible.

Then, a movement from the downed boat caught his eye. Oh shit. Another man—another Bot—was crawling out of the bowels of the ship. He extended a hand to someone behind him. Shit, shit, shit. There were more of them.

There were five specialists (no, shit, four) on the island. Two remained with Liao, watching this unholy scene. Liao looked through his scope at the Bots' faces and he knew that they were doing the very same math; the odds had turned on them and there was no way off this island. The tide wouldn't change for hours. They had their electro-prods but nothing else, nothing but their bare hands against the onslaught.

Liao switched his communication streams. "You get the backup here right now," he said, "or I'll have your goddamn head on a spike."

———o———

Physically, there was nothing about the other Bot that reminded Ebert of Avon. Where Avon had been tall and reedy, the other Bot—who told him softly that his name was Parker—was compact and dense. His face was very full, even slightly pudgy. Where Avon had been so pale as to be translucent,

Parker had very dark skin, very even in tone, like the matte side of a ribbon. He was not so ghostly or consumptive-looking. On the street, no one would even turn to look at Parker as he passed by.

But there was something about the both of them, an aura of fragility, perhaps a certain soft-spoken strangeness. Whatever it was, it made Ebert reach out to him on the aerial transport over to the island and it made Ebert want to stick close to him when they were dumped in the middle of the melee.

Bots of all affiliations had swarmed the little island. At least it was fairly easy to make a distinction between the two of them. The military Bots were wearing uniforms, not quite fatigues, more under-stated than that, but uniforms all the same. Thick khaki-style pants and black shirts. The outsider Bots were wearing all manner of street clothes.

They were also the ones winning, at least by Ebert's count.

"Come with me," he said to Parker, linking hands with him and beginning to run as soon as they hit the beach. Parker had stumbled along with him. Not, seemingly, out of any particular desire to escape but rather because he didn't seem to have any idea what else to do. Perhaps that was what had drawn Ebert to him, a certain kind of lost bemusement, someone who needed to be led or else they would only wander.

Ebert, however, had a plan. As he understood it, he could not be faulted for performing his duty exactly as directed. He was to find Edmond West. He had not been instructed to engage in combat with anyone. He had, in fact, been told to avoid that very situation.

The relative lack of pressure inside his skull as he ran confirmed that he had assessed the situation correctly. Having done away with the issue of the kill switch, the only thing left to do was to avoid any of the combatants who might be thinking about attacking them.

There was no oversight on the island. No leader barking orders. The military Bots were all obeying the terrible pain inside their heads. The outsider Bots were cutting them down like wheat during the harvest. Everywhere Ebert looked, small groups of Bots were struggling with one another. The island was not particularly large, Ebert estimate it was roughly four miles around and there was little in the way of places to hide. The Bots could do nothing but face one another.

The Refurbs were at a particular disadvantage. They had to get in close to effectively use their only weapon and so they left themselves vulnerable to a hammer strike. Essentially, they had to strike down the outsider Bots on the very first try because there would not be a second try.

Everywhere, the ground was littered with bodies. It was surprisingly sterile. Most of them had no obvious wounds and if there was blood, it was in drips and drops, not floods. They looked as though they had stretched out on the warm sand for an early morning nap. Ebert knew, however, that inside their skulls it was a different story altogether, a bloody ruin of what had once been the most advanced machine the world had ever seen.

Edmond West was said to be living in an abandoned bunker near the top of the island. Ebert wasn't sure exactly where that bunker might be, but he knew up from down, so he led Parker in a generally upward direction.

Parker asked him no questions. He stared avidly at the prone bodies on the sand. He would have stopped to investigate them closer if Ebert had allowed it. "Come along, come along," Ebert said, pulling on his hand. For some reason, he had adopted a sing-song cadence, as though Parker were a child who needed to be cajoled and coddled. At some point, Parker had lost his electro-device. Perhaps he had never even brought it to the island at all. He didn't seem to notice the loss, or anything else for that matter. For all the fear his face showed, they might have simply been taking a particularly rapid and unappealing sight-seeing trip.

Ebert wondered how "refurbished" Parker was.

Avon, after all, had presumably been cleared for all manner of intense duty, a job that had broken him utterly. If Parker were too fragile for this work, who would have said so? Who would have protected him at risk to their own job? No one in the world, Ebert knew, cared about a Bot. Except, very occasionally, another Bot.

There was an unpleasant smell in the air. It dominated the natural smells of the trees and the salt seawater. A burning, electric smell. Probably produced by those wicked prods meeting with flesh. Some of the military Bots were getting a bit of their own back, then.

Though he was surrounded on all sides by death, Ebert had to admit that this was the best he had felt since before his capture. It was as though a kindly universe had allowed him to travel back to that pivotal moment in the Belgian coffee shop and whisk Avon away to safety. He could do what he should have done then, what he would have done, had he not allowed his own fear to cripple him.

Ebert never saw Avon again. He saw dozens of other Refurbs, but never Avon. Avon did not come back to the lab.

But now he had a chance again to be brave for someone else.

"There's a path," Parker told him, interrupting his reverie. It was the first time Parker had actually spoken to Ebert. His voice was deep and level and that surprised Ebert. He had been expecting something more like Avon's dreamy murmur, not decisive, though muted tones.

Parker was also correct; there was a thin ribbon of beaten-down earth. It zigzagged up the island's primary hill. It almost certainly led to Edmond West's hideaway.

It was the path that inevitably fucked them.

Ebert should have found some way to generally pursue Edmond West without actually getting anywhere near him. He might have expected that the outsider Bots would be covering all entrances to the

West's compound. Of course they would be, they were here to protect their maker, after all.

For a moment, he hoped that he and Parker might have discovered the path before anyone else, that they might slip in silently while everyone else was fighting.

He felt the attack first as a wrenching from his hand. But, this time, he did not let go.

Parker's falling body pulled him down to the ground, but Ebert held on fast, as though their fingers had been glued together, interlaced. Parker made a stuttering noise, perhaps an attempt at speech (goodbyes?) or possibly just the sort of involuntary sound someone makes when blood compresses their brain into a gray smear.

Again, Ebert found himself kneeling next to someone he had promised himself he would protect, utterly unable to do anything for them. When he looked at Parker, he could not see the wound from the hammer's blow. He couldn't see anything at all. It seemed suddenly that Parker had no face at all. He wasn't Avon, he wasn't Parker, he was just a blank of misery.

For a split second, Ebert felt a surge of anger at the other Bot. How dare he die? How dare he get his skull cracked with Ebert so close to rescuing him and redeeming himself? Almost instantly, the absurdity of this idea dawned on him and, incredibly, Ebert started to laugh.

"Ebert?" came a woman's voice from the air far above him.

He was still holding Parker's hand. Was it still Parker's hand when the other Bot was, by now, almost certainly gone? Was it just a hand now, waiting to be harvested and recycled to become someone's new skin and bone? He turned to face the voice.

For the second time in as many minutes, Ebert found himself laughing at something that wasn't actually very funny at all. It was Sheba, looming above him with a hardware-store hammer in her hand, like some sort of low-rent version of Thor the Thunder God.

"You're here," she said and she sounded so terribly demoralized. Ebert thought about how it must be for her, cutting down Refurbs whom she knew to be acting under the constraint of their kill switches. Some of them might even have been friends. Like him.

"Hey, Sheba," Ebert said weakly.

"You can't go up there, Ebert," she said, gesturing towards the path.

Ebert shrugged his shoulders. "I can't not." In his head, the kill switch thrummed. It did not like him waiting here, wasting time. It looked a lot like cowardice which was spitting distance from rebellion. Ebert comforted himself with the knowledge that his pain would be ending very soon.

She nodded and they were silent together in their shared knowledge of what had to happen now.

"I'm sorry," Sheba said.

"I know," Ebert told her.

With some difficulty, he detangled his fingers from Parker's and stood up slowly. He reached out his hand for Sheba's. She took it. "It's okay," he said and he mustered up the biggest smile he could.

Her eyes were so infinitely sad.

It was the longest moment of stillness and silence he'd had since arriving on the island. It allowed him to pick out the sound of shouts, of babbles, of electricity burning through bodies. He tried to pick something, anything else out of the cacophony. Even just the sounds of waves somewhere meeting the shore. Even just the sound of the wind moving the greenery.

Ebert was still listening for something else, something more, when Sheba moved.

Her hand darted towards him like a striking snake and then there was a little bloom of discomfort at his throat. A burst of something bright and the great darkness once again.

———O———

There was something almost imperial about Hart as she sat on her makeshift chair, constructed from a broken concrete block. A bent stick of rebar served as an armrest and she pillowed her chin on her hand, looking down into the green oblivion of the island below them.

"How long have you been doing it?" Edmond asked her.

Every once in a while, they would hear a terribly truncated shout. Something like a guttural scream.

"I started in Michigan," Hart admitted. "I made some cultures from the samples I took of the dead girl."

Edmond did not allow himself to wonder how this was possible. He knew very well how it was possible. He had been living underneath a cloud since Michigan. Since before Michigan. Since they had fled the lab, even. Hart could have cobbled together a fire-breathing dragon from wood scraps and turkey leftovers and he wouldn't have noticed.

"Jeb doesn't just bring supplies for me, does he?"

Hart shook her head.

"How many did you make?" Edmond asked. The fighters below them seemed pretty evenly matched, which suggested far more non-military Bots than Edmond would have thought possible.

"Seven," she answered. "But I don't know how many they made."

"They're making more themselves?" Edmond couldn't keep the panic out of his voice. Hart turned to look at him, surprised.

"Of course," she said, "how else are we supposed to preserve our population. Isn't it the most natural instinct of any creature, to reproduce itself?"

Edmond sat down at her right hand on the dusty floor. "You are not natural," he said.

"I know." Hart's voice came from far away and above him.

"Are you sorry that they are here?" Hart asked and she sounded generally uncertain. For the first time in a long while, she seemed to be looking to him for direction. Down below them, something horrible was happening. Edmond wasn't sure what he was sorry for or what he was grateful for. Except for the leaves on the trees. He was grateful for the leaves on the trees and how they obscured everything underneath.

"No," he said, "I'm not sorry."

It occurred to him then (though surely he should have realized it before) that Hart must have known last night that all this would happen, that these people were coming to . . . rescue them? She had known and she had kept that knowledge from him, another scar hidden by the things she wore.

"Did you bring them here?" Edmond asked her.

"I didn't ask them to come," Hart said. "But . . . I knew they might. They needed to be told." Of course, she had a point. The Army would not quietly recede after addressing the problem of Edmond and Hart. They would pursue and recapture any non-sanctioned Bots, especially if they found out that still more were being fabricated all the time.

Still, it unnerved him to think of Hart as a

strategic animal, some commander marshalling her forces. When they left the lab, it had been violent and it had been terrible, but it had been the two of them fleeing a force obviously more powerful. There had been something virtuous in it, the pair of them existing only for one another. Edmond wasn't at all sure he was ready to be on one side of a war.

And yet that's exactly what was happening, down there underneath the green leaves. And this was just the first battle, Edmond realized. The first battle of his new war.

EIGHT

TRIAGE

ISLA REDONDA, MEXICO. NOVEMBER, 2045

It had not occurred to Edmond that there would be wounded. The military had undoubtedly done everything they could to make their Bots as durable as possible. To incapacitate them usually meant complete destruction.

He had not seen the taser devices before, though they seemed clever. Maybe Janelle had thought of that? It was the kind of solution that Janelle often proposed; it was both pragmatic and humane, designed to save the Bot and the investment of time and resources that the Bot represented.

They had never looked more doll-like to him than they did like this, inert and deactivated, limbs akimbo on the uneven ground. Hart moved among them easily, a strange Florence Nightingale, pausing momentarily beside each one to examine the body in detail. She was looking for the telltale twin burn marks, like a vampire's bite.

The others ones—the ones who would never wake—appeared almost untouched, at least at first glance. If one looked closer, they might occasionally see a small depression along the side of the face, perhaps the bluish-black of a just-antemortem bruise. All the blood rushing uselessly to the surface.

Edmond walked amongst them as well, but he did not bend down to minister to them as Hart did. In a way, it was fascinating. Edmond was looking at the future of his ideas. He was looking at all his dreams, these dead dolls.

To the naked eye, they all looked very similar, but Edmond could actually spot significant distinctions between them. Some were clearly more advanced than others. Some of them had not had the benefit of top-of-the-line materials (or possibly of a truly visionary creator). They looked more like the crude automatons that Edmond had set out to surpass and replace all those years ago.

Others were incredibly detailed, almost perfect imitations of humanity. Though, he flattered himself that none of them were quite as good as Hart. Perhaps it was harder to judge, though, when they were deactivated. In this state, they would always lack her spark.

Few of the Bots who had come to their rescue remained standing and alert. Those that did stuck close to Hart and had not yet addressed Edmond. They didn't seem to know how to deal with him at all. Or else they just didn't find him nearly as interesting as they did Hart. He wondered which of them were her creations alone and which of them had been generated by others out to propagate their species. A lone voice in the back of his head, small and long-neglected, wondered if the Bot-made Bots were better than Edmond's own.

They looked at Hart with something approaching

the spiritual in their affect. Their eyes followed her wherever she went and her every suggestion was immediately enacted. One, a large blonde woman, seemed to have affixed herself permanently to Hart's elbow as though she were gunning for the nonexistent position of Grand Vizier to Hart's Empress of Bots.

Edmond wondered for the first time what was to happen now. There had been so much to take in after the fighting. The bodies, the chaos, even the doomed watercrafts sunk into the sand. Would they all . . . just leave now? Go back to wherever it was that they were . . . from? Stationed? Edmond didn't know how far this extended. It didn't seem that Hart had been instructing them or directing their movements from afar, but Edmond had missed so much. He felt as though he were awakening after the kind of sleep that eats a night, a day, countless hours, and leaves the sleeper out of time and place.

Hart lingered beside one body. She settled back

on her haunches and balanced her chin on two hands thoughtfully. The body before her was particularly hard done by. Someone had gotten a very good blow, or else had kept hitting the Bot when she was down. The right side of her face was a crater, though an unnervingly bloodless one. Edmond saw immediately what had happened: someone hit her hard enough to dent her internal skeletal structure, but the skin over it had held fast. Synthetic skin was particularly resistant to blunt force trauma, but it performed less well with puncture wounds and slices. Edmond remembered that from the multiple rounds of testing.

Either way, it was more than enough to burst the ersatz aneurysm that the military was implanting in all of their units. The girl in Michigan had died a long, slow death, a seep of blood that slowly crushed her brain tissue, neurons firing off in a wild panic before, finally, she succumbed.

These Bots went quickly. Undoubtedly, that was by design. The kill switch was not engineered to be a torture device (though it could, in fact, be used in that way) it was designed to give the Bots a clean death.

And yet, looking around him, Edmond had never felt less clean in his life. It was enough to make him want to walk out into the ocean. Just walk, until the water closed over his head and erased him from the world. The world would undoubtedly be a better place if he were carefully elided from it. A blank space where someone might start over and build something infinitely better.

Hart was touching the dead Bot's crushed skull. She grasped the woman's chin in her hand and turned the head slightly, facing the undamaged side of her head upwards. With two delicate fingers, Hart pried the Bot's eye open. The sclera was clear with little sign of the cloudiness that was so distinctive of deceased humans. It would come in time, Edmond knew. In this, as in most things, Bots were only a little bit better than humans.

Edmond crouched down beside her.

"We could use this," Hart said.

Edmond took several issues with that sentence. *We*, *use*, *this*—all presented problems for him. "What do you mean?" he said.

"Her eye," Hart said. "It's an incredibly complex mechanism. And it's intact right here. It just needs to be reconnected to a working brain."

"You want this woman to become an organ donor?"

Hart looked at him and her face brightened. For a moment, she reminded him of those first few days in the lab when she had been hungry for any little piece of the world. "Is that what they're called?" she asked.

"For humans," Edmond said, "yeah, that's what they're called." Once, he had been able to answer all of her questions so easily. Once, his answers had delighted her, opening up another aspect of being alive. Now, he showed her the mechanics of death, the intricacies of destruction.

Hart closed the woman's eye again. "We need

to figure out how to preserve these people. We can save them. Parts of them."

Edmond hadn't even noticed the blonde woman drifting up behind him. For someone that generally large, she moved as silently as any tiny woodland critter. Hart looked at her, over Edmond's shoulder. "We need to save as much of them as possible," she told the blonde woman, and Edmond had not misheard her or imagined. It was an order.

———o———

It came upon with a cold clarity and Janelle almost couldn't find it in herself to feel afraid or dejected or angry or any of the other emotions that Janelle thought she would surely feel when her career went swirling down the drain.

Instead, she felt nothing at all. It was like an anesthesia of the heart. It was all she could do to stare directly at General Liao and attempt to make the correct sort of facial expressions.

"Please tell me," he was saying, "that this was not as easily preventable as it appeared to be. Please tell me we didn't leave millions of dollars lying on that beach because you didn't think to ... to ... " Liao cast about, looking for his easy solution, " ... give them a better fucking helmet?"

That frozen feeling had started slowly while Janelle had watched the update stream on the mission. At first, she had been confused, then alarmed, then horrified. Finally, she felt a wave of something like admiration. It wasn't as though they had never imagined the idea of external pressure causing the kill switches to detonate prematurely. In fact, they had tried something very similar on testing units, but apparently they hadn't realized how very delicate and precise the whole process was. A tiny weakness, relative to the rest of a Bot's physiology, a little area of thinned-out bone above the right ear. Strike anywhere else and they were Teflon. Strike there and they were a useless pile of wreckage.

The only thing Janelle could think of was that the opposition had somehow seen this peculiarity of the kill-switch tech in action somewhere. But they had full data on all kill-switch-enabled Bots and none of them had recorded a rupture outside of controlled detonations in the laboratory itself. And they were so confident, smug, even, with their hardware store arsenal.

"We didn't see spontaneous ruptures in any of the laboratory tests—"

"They weren't spontaneous. Someone smashed them in the fucking head with a hammer."

If Janelle had been consumed with righteous anger, if she had been vigorously defending herself on the off-chance that she might be able to still save her job, she might have been forgiven some insubordination. But she wasn't angry. She was tired, exhausted, even. Too tired to bullshit.

"Sir, we didn't know this would happen because we didn't have enough time to put the units through a responsible amount of testing. We rushed the implementation process and we pushed the Refurbs into the field before most of them were ready. And we did that because we rushed the initial rollout and we did that because Edmond West had you all scared shitless."

A fear that, as it turned out, was justified. Not only was Edmond West smarter than almost any one of them as individuals, but he was not mired in bureaucratic hierarchy, allowing him to work small and quick, the way guerrillas and terrorists had for thousands of years. Except these guerrillas were almost impossible to kill.

"You can lay this at my door," Janelle continued, "and I'm betting that you will. But you fucked yourself on this one, General, and we both know that."

Janelle knew that court-martial was not out of the question in this situation. She also knew that every salty thing she said right now only made that option look more and more attractive to Liao. But since the age of fifteen, she had poured her whole self into the dream of this laboratory, this white coat, and these responsibilities. She had never wanted to be anything other than a roboticist, and she had never prepared to do anything else. Her career was blowing up around her and if, afterwards, she spent her days in a jail cell, then what of it? It wasn't like she had some other plan B.

She hadn't been a civilian for more than twenty years. She didn't even remember what she used to be good at before she was so good at building advanced weaponry.

And all this time, Liao was silent. He was giving her what she thought of as his recruitment look. It always put Janelle in the mind of that jackal-headed Egyptian god that people used to believe judged the souls of the dead against the weight of a feather.

"So what?" Liao said. "You're just going to cut and run now? This is my mess, just as you say, but it's your mess too. Aren't you going to help me clean it up?"

It was far more than ninety-four hours this time, though Ebert himself had no way of knowing that. He knew only that, this time, when he woke up, it was to cool darkness, rather than the fluorescent light of the laboratory.

In those moments before the power of speech returned to him, a strange image flittered through his mind, a story he'd read once, before he had even left the laboratory. Back when he was still learning how to be human, as though that were a thing that was possible. As though that were a thing that was desirable.

It was an Edgar Allan Poe story he had found during his online dalliances, "A Premature Burial," and it involved just that. There was something about the quality of the darkness—it seemed textured and heavy, as though a lack of light could have a weight all its own—that made him wonder for one unrestrained second whether he had somehow been buried underneath the ground.

But that was stupid, because no one would bury a Bot. His component parts were far too valuable (not quite as valuable as they were altogether, but still). No, he was alive and alone and breathing air above the ground.

His first word was more like a rusty croak. He meant to say something along the lines of, "Excuse me, where am I?" He managed something more like, "Euurgh."

That was enough, though, to summon someone from that soupy darkness. A warm hand grasped his and he was suddenly made aware of his body. Hands. He had hands. They were lying uselessly at his sides. He flexed his fingers inside the other person's handclasp.

"Hi," the voice was chipper and youthful. Ebert swallowed hard.

"Hi," he answered. It still sounded like a creaking whisper, but it was at least a recognizable word.

"You're safe," said the voice. "This isn't the Army. This isn't the lab."

The hand gave his a squeeze.

"Where am I, then?" Ebert asked.

"You're with Hart's people," the voice answered immediately. "The Bot Resistance Force."

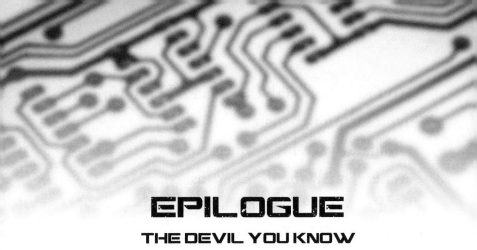

EPILOGUE
THE DEVIL YOU KNOW
San Domenica, California. November, 2045

Kadence would never see the inside of a prison, if they found her, if they caught her. At least, not a real prison. Maybe one of those black-site places in, like, Moldova or somewhere. Some hellhole where they locked you up until your bones turned to dust.

She knew that, technically, that wasn't supposed to happen to American citizens. But she figured that they would make an exception for her. For this. And what was this? It was, as she had increasingly realized, treason. Did they still execute people by firing squad for treason, or would it be the snakebite of a needle and straps on all her limbs?

Kadence followed the information from the island skirmish along with everyone else in the laboratory. It was all she could do not to show panic all over her face as the updates rolled in, each one more dire than the last.

At least no one was asking her to talk. She didn't think she could keep the shaking out of her voice. Instead, everyone seemed to have been struck dumb with horror. At one point, Kadence thought she heard Eun-hye stifle a sob.

Oddly enough, that relaxed Kadence slightly. *It would be natural to be upset,* she told herself, *a terrible thing has happened.* The continued viability of the robotics department was on the line now. Of course Kadence would be a little panicked. A young careerist like herself, she would probably be hyperventilating and desperately trying to plot her next leap.

But it was, ultimately, the panic of others that reassured her the most. Each of them was grappling with their own private realizations of how much they had to lose, the precipice they didn't even know they were standing upon. How could they be expected to monitor Kadence's emotional state when they were trying to manage their own?

Kadence wanted to leave almost immediately. As soon as reports of the hammers came in, she knew what would happen. What was happening, thousands of miles away. She wanted to minimize her time here, amongst her coworkers and their—admittedly limited—scrutiny. But she also simply didn't want to sit through what she knew was coming.

But, Good Kadence, the Kadence who never betrayed her country and her coworkers, she would not have known. She would have experienced each little shock with the rest of them, her confident optimism transmuting slowly into despondency. She would not have kept looking at the door with longing.

Kadence tried hard to be Good Kadence, to creep into her skin. Occasionally there would be whole moments when she would truly feel like that girl again. It was as though she were channelling her confusion and fear like a voice from the Other Side. She wondered if that was what it was like to be a spy: to convince yourself that you were fundamentally a different person. Maybe that was where it had to start.

Kadence didn't want to be a spy but not as much as she didn't want to be a prisoner. And so she waited it out, until the bitter end, which she had expected from the beginning. It was a total rout, a failure in every aspect. It would probably cost every person in this room their job.

No one had spoken during the mission and no one spoke now that it was over. But there was a change, somehow, in the silence. It had felt natural before, even light. Now it was layered with expectation. Someone had to say something.

Kadence knew it couldn't be her.

She wondered if it would appear natural for her

to run for the door. She thought she could produce some very realistic tears right now, if she needed to.

A brief, dull tone interrupted her strategic reverie. She glanced down at her flex-tablet, curled up on the table before her. She wasn't supposed to take personal calls at work under normal circumstances, let alone during a critical operation that intimately involved her department. So she had entirely failed to notice that her sister Ayleh had called her nineteen times in the last forty minutes.

Kadence flicked through her various messaging services, each of them blazing red with unread correspondence. Her sister again, her messages like a stuttering poem:

call me

call me

call me when you get this.

call me now.

answer your phone

your fucking phone, answer your fucking phone

call me

call me. where are you.

"I'm sorry," Kadence said, scooping up the flex-tablet and tucking it into her pocket. "There's an emergency at home."

She was grateful for the excuse, but she needn't have bothered. The rest of the lab barely looked up as she left. They were all sitting alone with their fears.

Kadence waited until she was in the parking lot before she called her sister back.

"Hey, sorry," she began, as soon as Ayleh picked up the line.

"Mom shot herself," her sister said, before Kadence could get out another word.

For a moment, there were no words. There weren't even thoughts.

" . . . What? How?" Kadence stammered finally. "Was it an accident?"

She hadn't even known her parents had a gun, let alone knew how to use it. Maybe Mom had gotten paranoid now that Dad was so sick?

"No, no, no," Ayleh said. Kadence noticed for the first time how thick her sister's voice sounded. It was as though she were recovering from a bad cold. "She put down a tarp . . . she put Dodger in his crate . . ."

"What do you mean? A tarp?"

"She shot herself!" Ayleh cried, anguished. "She tried to fucking kill herself, Kadence."

Ten seconds of nothingness, and then: "She *tried*?"

"We're at the hospital," Ayleh said. "She's still in surgery."

"Which hospital?" Kadence demanded.

Ayleh told her the address and explained in a surprisingly normal tone which parking lot was for visitors. She had gotten in touch with their other siblings, she said, they were all en route but, right now, it was just Ayleh and their father.

The next few minutes seemed to proceed in a series of snapshot flashes. Somehow, Kadence found herself behind the wheel of her car with no memory of how she had gotten there.

A red light, and she was acutely aware of her breathing.

Turning the wheel carefully into the visitors' lot.

Sitting for a moment, the engine cooling in the dark of the parking structure.

The deep, terrible part of her that felt relief when, just for a little while, the Bots program was not her biggest problem.

The shuddering breath she took as she opened her door.

The white gleam of the hospital ahead of her.

The vanishing sound of her footsteps on concrete.

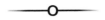

"All of this is fixable," Gina told her at their first meeting after the fiasco in Mexico.

Kadence couldn't pick between the plenitude

of nasty replies that immediately sprang to mind. "You must know something I don't know," she said instead, as evenly as possible. SennTech was her only bridge left, she wasn't going anywhere near it with a lit match.

"Of course." Anyone else, and it would have seemed like a terribly smug reply. But on Gina, with her effervescent grin, it merely appeared tone deaf. It occurred to Kadence, though, that Gina could not be nearly so daffy as she appeared.

"Look, the kill switch needs to be redesigned. That's clear." Gina gave Kadence her laughable version of a hard-ass stare. "Some real big flaws there, huh?"

Kadence just barely resisted the urge to point out that she had told Gina to bring Emily back in as soon as she was showing signs of disorientation and scattered thinking. Back in the lab, Kadence could have examined the girl up close, maybe corrected the problem before they gave Edmond West a command performance of their Achille's Heel in action. If she had any actual power at SennTech, she could have sidestepped the entire problem. Instead, she was just a resource. They were going to pick the information out of her, like meat from a bone, and then leave the rest behind.

"But we can address all of that. We haven't been materially set back." Unlike (Gina did not need to add) the Army, which was out millions in materials and labor.

"Also," Gina gave Kadence her most conspiratorial grin, as though she were about to tell her where all the Christmas presents were hidden, "we have a little ace up our sleeve."

Gina offered a pregnant pause. She seemed barely able to contain her excitement. There was something about it that Kadence found almost physically nauseating. A grown-ass woman acting like an overeager child. "We imprinted every part of Emily—of all the SennTech units—with GPS mapping. On the cellular level."

Kadence just looked at her. So what? They could

go retrieve poor Emily's bones from Bumfuck, Michigan?

Gina's smile dipped only slightly. This was clearly not the reaction she had been reaching for. "That means," she said slowly, leadenly, as though Kadence were stupid, "if Edmond West keeps even a single cell of hers around, we can track his movements."

The little woman reached forward and clasped Kadence's hand. Kadence was never going to get used to this sort of thing from her. "He'll never be out of our sight again. You see? I told you everything was going to be okay. Emily was a success, you know. She did just what we needed her to do."

If she got any closer, surely she would notice how Kadence stank like bleach and urine. Like hospital. She'd come from her mother's recovery room straight to the SennTech building. There was blood on her cuff. She had been holding her mother's hand where they had inserted the IVs. One needle had shifted around and produced a little red, running blood. It went from her mother's body to Kadence's skin to Kadence's clothes. It probably wouldn't wash out.

Kadence had not thought, on the ride over, about her mother. She couldn't. She couldn't even try. The badness seemed too big, the future too impossible. She couldn't get her mind around it.

Her mother was alive in her hospital bed and she would probably stay there. She had been so careful, she put on her favorite shoes and her nicest cardigan. She spread the tarp out in the backyard so no one would have to clean up after her. She made their father a series of meals and froze them ahead of time. She waited until he was at a doctor's appointment so he would not try to stop her.

Then she put the pistol she'd purchased on credit to her right temple and fired.

So perfect. So carefully planned. But she could not micromanage a bullet. It went where it wished, debilitating but not destroying. It had torn up her brain. The doctors were uncertain what, if any, mental faculties she would be able to recover. Right now, she was a "full-time-care situation."

Kadence couldn't look directly at her face, swollen and grotesque. Her mother who was so courteous to them all. How could she have imagined that this would make life easier for any of them? How could she have left them alone with their ever-increasing burdens?

"I need more money," Kadence said, staring directly at Gina. She wasn't thinking about bridges and fire. She was thinking about hospice, about recovery, about in-home nurses and repeat surgeries. She was thinking about her siblings, three of whom hadn't even finished college. If she was going to sell her soul, she couldn't afford to do it for a penny less than top dollar.

"Of course," Gina said. "By the way, we were so sorry to hear about your mother."

That pulled Kadence up short. There was no way that SennTech should have "heard about her mother." Kadence had never, in fact, mentioned her family at all. True, her father's situation was a matter of public record and it was likely a big part of the reason that they had approached her in the first place. But her mother had only been in the hospital a matter of hours. Was someone . . . following her? Watching her? Had someone in the hospital passed them information?

"Thank you," Kadence said uneasily.

"In fact, we were thinking about offering you a raise commensurate with your new appointment," Gina said, breezing past Kadence's discomfort.

Kadence gave her a confused look.

"We want you to make us something very special. Someone very special. A . . . companion, uniquely suited to a specific person."

That sounded more like a commercial assignment, not the sort of thing that Kadence was brought on board to do and the skepticism must have showed in her face because Gina added, "Trust me, this will be a challenge. But don't worry, we'll give you a full dossier on the young lady and you have plenty of time to develop someone just perfect for her."

Gina snapped her fingers as though she had forgotten something in an oven somewhere. "You may have met her, actually. She's about your age. Miss Shannon Liao?"